UPTOWN DREAMS

Also by Kelli London

Boyfriend Season

The Break-Up Diaries, Vol. 1 (with Ni-Ni Simone)

Published by Kensington Publishing Corp.

UPTOWN DREAMS

Kelli London

Dafina KTeen Books
KENSINGTON PUBLISHING CORP.
www.kensingtonbooks.com/KTeen

DAFINA KTEEN BOOKS are published by

Kensington Publishing Corp.
119 West 40th Street
New York, NY 10018

ISBN-13: 978-0-7582-6128-1
ISBN-10: 0-7582-6128-4

First Printing: December 2011
10   9   8   7   6   5   4   3   2   1

Printed in the United States of America

For all the dreamers of the world:
You are now holding someone's dream realized. Let it
serve as proof that yours, too, can become real. Let your
belief pave the way for achievement. Be confident that
you can move your dreams from downtown (deep in
your imagination) to uptown (into real life) so everyone
else can enjoy, celebrate, and recognize your
achievement. Never stop and never give up. Breathe life
into your dreams as they breathe life into you.
Cheers to you!

ACKNOWLEDGMENTS

A special thanks to my princess and princes: T, CII, K, and J. Without your love, patience, guidance, and encouragement, my works wouldn't be or make it to completion. I love you all! Muaah—> (me kissing you, individually and collectively).

JH, thanks for cheering me on, being in my corner, and never letting me down. CLP loves you completely and endlessly—literally, figuratively, and every other good word that ends with a *lee* sound.☺

For my family and friends who so willingly overlook and forgive my missing-in-action while I'm writing, I thank you.

A huge kudos and many hugs to my dream team young adult consultants in New York, Atlanta, and Philadelphia: Rukiya "Kiki" Murray, Alakea Woods, Josh "UnconQUErable" Woods, Chris Ferreras, and Eligio "E." (Zap) Bailey. You are all priceless!

Thanks to my fellow writers who offer wonderful teen readers an escape and entertainment. I am proud to be a part of the movement.

Selena James, you are a consummate professional, and I can't thank you enough. Your dedication and sharp eye are incredible and impeccable. Every writer should be so fortunate!

For my readers, I truly and humbly thank you with all of my heart. You're incredible, appreciated, and top of tops. Let's rock the world together!

From Kelli

When I was a little girl, I was asked to write something for a school employee who was retiring. I was only six-years-old, but like many children, I'd been creative for a long, long time☺, so I knew without a doubt that I could do it. I had done it before. Constantly, I had invented "friends" who'd turned into characters who, in my mind, were real because they lived in my imagination. These imaginary people spoke, thought, felt, started trouble and even saved the world. They were, in essence, super-heroes who could do anything they wanted—*every*thing I wanted. At that time, I was too young to realize that my "friends" were the beginnings of books, the start of my career as a fiction writer. All I knew then was I'd created and enjoyed them, and kept company with them until their stories had been told. In short, I had a dream—a real, live, living, breathing dream that I knew I had to re-alize. And I did. That's why I want you to know that you, too, can make your dreams come true. All it'll take is a bit of hard work, dedication, and belief.

Take care. Be strong. Love yourself. I'll be cheering you on.

Your girl,
Kells
KelliLondon.com

WELCOME TO
HARLEM, N.Y.

Population: 215,753
Area: 3.871 square miles
DREAMS: UNLIMITED

HARLEM ACADEMY OF CREATIVE AND
PERFORMING ARTS
(CAPA)

*Dreams aren't meant to be dreamt. Dreams are
meant to be realized.*

ROLL CALL

LA-LA NOLAN

"I don't sing, I sang."

"Lexus and Mercedes, get off my feet before you get murked!" I warned my two sisters, shaking my legs one at a time, trying to break loose from their three- and four-year-old grips. It was too early for a foot ride, and I needed to get out the door and make tracks to get to school.

"Please, La-La," they sang in unison. "Foot ride. Foot ride. Foot ride!" they chanted.

"I. Said. Get. Off." I shuffled my feet one at a time, enunciating each word while alternately swinging my legs back and forth. Reaching down, I pressed my hand against Mercedes's forehead and pushed it with all my might.

"Boom-Kesha," she yelled out to our mother. "La-La murked me!"

Her snitching really set my fire, so I swished my legs one at a time as if I were punting a football. Lexus was my first successful attempt. With a harder kick and powerful shake and swoop, I managed to break her grasp, then watched in semi-terror as she slid across the linoleum and connected with the painted concrete wall. The top of her head met the dent-proof wall first, colliding with a thump that I was sure would make her cry.

"Wee!" she shouted, surprising me, then jumped up and came back for another turn.

"Me too. Me too," Mercedes pleaded. "Slide me, too."

I pointed at Lexus like that Celie chick from that old *Color Purple* movie when she gave that ancient Mister dude that Hoodoo sign. Lexus froze in her tracks. Four out of six of my siblings were terrified of that hand gesture because they believed everything they saw on TV, and they were sure it was magic of some sorts. Well, I'd made them believe I had that power because it worked to my benefit whenever they rode my nerves. "'Whatever you done to me,'" I threatened, parroting Celie's line from the movie, making my voice deep and stretching my eyes wide.

Lexus ran out screaming like she was on fire; then Mercedes started to cry, releasing her slob and nose mucus dams.

"Ill." Her nose and the sides of her mouth were running with clear and yellow gook. "Now you better get up. I don't want your cooties on my clothes."

She unwound herself from my leg, got off my foot, and whooshed away like a fire truck, screaming down the hall like a siren. "Cooties-cooties-cooties!"

"Henrietta!" my mother's voice carried into the room. "Henrietta?"

Lexus came back to the door, peeking her head in. Then Alize, Remi, and Queen showed up, followed by King, crawling his way through their legs. I shook my head. My siblings were beautiful and smart, though many would never know it because my mother had cursed them. She had named them after liquor and luxury cars, or given them aristocratic titles like we hailed from a monarchy instead of a New York housing project. But, the truth of the matter was, she'd done what so many others do: named her children after things she'd wanted but would never have.

"Henrietta! Heifer, I know you hear me," Boom-Kesha's—I mean Momma's—raspy Newport voice floated into the room.

"You better answer her, La-La," Remi warned. She was thirteen and ten months younger than me, but so much older than anyone else in the apartment. She'd been sick for months, diagnosed with cancer, and it was hellish, making her grow up faster than she should've. I would've done anything to take it away from her. Remi tightened up the headscarf she wore to hide her hair, which had begun to fall out in big clean patches. "Her panties have been in a twist ever since she woke up, something about the city cutting her benefits. Like we was gonna be able to get welfare forever." She crossed her arms and sucked her teeth.

"You okay?" I asked, ignoring my mother calling me. I didn't like the coloring of Remi's skin. It was starting to gray like my grandfather's before he died.

Remi nodded. "I'm good. I just wish I had hair like yours. It seems too strong to fall out."

"Henrietta!" Boom-Kesha boomed again.

I touched my head, wishing I could give it to Remi. "Well, I wish I had your teeth. They're so pretty and white—so straight."

"Henrietta!"

"Henrietta? Don't shu 'ear you mami talking to ju?" Paco, my mother's bootleg, pretending-to-be-Spanish boyfriend, poked his head into the bedroom and asked in his borrowed Spanglish. The man was crazy. Just because his skin was light and sun-kissed, his hair was straight black and silky, and people mistook him for Dominican, he'd reinvented himself as one. He even walked around with a Dominican flag wrapped around his head at the Puerto Rican Day parade, complaining that New York didn't give the Dominicans a holiday. But, I guess—for him—it was cool. If he could pretend to be a real full-grown man and get away with it, he could lie about being anything else.

I looked at Paco, pointing to my ears. *"Que?"* I asked him *what?* in Spanish, pretending to buy into his fabricated heritage.

"Oh. Ju ears stopped up this morning? Up giving singing lessons all night to get free tutoring, chica? No problemo. I splain to ju mami for ju."

I pasted a fake smile on my face and smirked a thank-you. Everybody in the house had bought my lie. I had them all thinking that I was receiving tutoring so I could keep up in the fancy performing-arts school I'd been offered a full scholarship to after the director heard me singing on the train. The Harlem Academy of Creative and Performing Arts, aka CAPA. It was a school that was supposed to make me and my mother Boom-Kesha's dreams come true; it was going to help make me a star and help her milk some money from some bourgeois art society that dished out funds to kids like me—teenagers who showed talent and promise, and didn't mind extra training to get into highfalutin Julliard, the other It school for college students that had recently showed interest in my voice. My mother was undoubtedly going to smoke and drink up the "extra" money, or use it on whatever her real addiction was. All I wanted was to get my teeth fixed, which was the reason I'd told them the tutoring lie. Really, I'd been hanging out in the adult singing spots in Greenwich Village, scouting singers I could one day sing backup for and, hopefully, stack my money for an orthodontist. "Good lookin', Paco," I said, grabbing my book bag and heading to the door.

"Henrietta!" my mom's voice stopped me before I could put my hand on the knob.

"La-La, La-La, La-La!" I sang to her. I don't know why I had to remind her of the name she crowned me with. She was the one who said I sang like a songbird and dubbed me La-La, as if I could've afforded one more reason for the kids to tease me. It was bad enough my teeth were raggedy, and I was so skinny the thick girls started calling me Anna—short for anorexic. I'd been jonesed about my lack of weight forever, but not my grill because I kept my mouth closed as much as possible.

"Make sure you bring a weapon with you, and don't take the elevator because the gangs have it sowed up. I don't want you to be a victim—you're my star."

No, I'm your paycheck. Your ticket out of the projects.

"Me, Paco, Alize, Remi, Lexus, Mercedes, Queen, and King will be waiting outside when you get home. 'Cause if that wench, Nakeeda, from last year wants it, we'll give it to her. I ain't above dusting a kid, and her raggedy mother too."

"Word, La-La," Remi added from behind my mother. "I may be sick, but I can get it in. I won't even have to put my hair in a ponytail 'cause ain't enough left to pull out," she teased, but I felt her pain.

I mouthed *I love you* to Remi, then feigned a smile and looked at my mother. Her intentions were good, but that's all they'd ever be—intentions. She really didn't have a desire to better herself or her family. We were living the project stereotype. I felt sorry for her and us, her children. It was sad that everyone, including my family, had started calling her Boom-Kesha, because every time someone looked up—Boom! Kesha was pregnant by a different man, then gave the child a ghetto first name and a different daddy's surname (except for me—I was named after my grandmother). What was worse was that my mother preferred to be called Boom-Kesha.

"I'm good. Cyd will be with me."

Cyd was my girl, my sister from a different mother. We were beyond best friends, and we rocked out—boys, parties, dreams, it didn't matter. And together, we were going to rock Harlem Academy, show 'em what we were made of, just like I planned to show Ziggy, the cute dude I'd met in the admissions office.

REESE ALLEN

"I'm a musician second, and a producer first."

5 A.M. *Five ay-em. Five o'clock in the morning! Is she serious?* I peeled open my eyelids and looked at the beaming red numbers, then closed them again. It was way too early for anything, especially getting up.

"C'mon, Reese!"

Clap. Clap.

"It's time to practice!"

Clap. Clap.

Ohmygod. Ohmygod. She was serious and in Mrs. Allen form like *whoa*. What was up with her waking me before sunrise and Sandman the wino's bedtime? I would've done anything to go back in time if high school was going to mean this.

Clap. Clap. Clap.

"Perfect practice makes perfect. Up-up-up!"

Oh, no. Not the triple claps. I knew what that meant. First slapping her hands together as loudly as possible, and now her hand was on my shoulder, shimmying me from side to side as if shaking me was gonna make me want to get up. I crossed my eyes, and cursed in my head. Was she certifiably crazy or just really enthused? I'd *just* gone to bed at midnight. Had just hit the pillow five stinking hours ago because she'd insisted that I practice cello, piano, violin, and the sax until *she* was satisfied. But I wasn't surprised, it was always about her. My life was hers.

I don't know how I got past her and her incessant clapping, but, somehow I managed to whir by her in a flash, but not before noticing she had a nametag pinned to her lapel. *Mrs. Allen, Director.* There was no way I was going to pull up to Harlem Academy with her. It was bad enough I had to attend the school she directed instead of the one I wanted to go to—Bronx Science, which was hard to get into, and where you needed to be borderline genius to be a student. I also didn't need anyone to know I was her daughter.

Before the shower's spray rained on the bathtub floor, I'd worked a shower cap around my bobby-pinned wrapped hair, sloshed a mask on my face, and stuck waterproof headphones in my ears. I'd played classical music last night; my mother's favorite. This morning, my choice: the tracks I'd been sneaking and working on be-hind her back—hip-hop and hardcore rap. The beats bumped in my ears loud enough to rattle my eardrums and allow the bass to vibrate my skeletal system. If Mommy Dearest could hear it, and knew I'd produced them with Blaze, my boyfriend she also knew nothing about, she'd topple to the floor. The music continued to take me away while I dressed.

"Reese, you've been in there almost an hour!" The boom of her fists shook the bathroom door, and I knew it was time to make an appearance.

With bobby pins removed, my hair flowed down to my elbows, cascading across my shoulders and hiding the small earbuds I'd stuck deep in the canals of my ears. I pulled out the piano bench in the living room, lifted the lid covering the ivory keys, sat down, and turned up my iPod all at once. Then I played. I straight grooved and allowed the piano to drown out the thump-thump-thump of the hip-hop that caressed my soul. Jay-Z, Drake, T.I., and Kanye all accompanied me as I stepped into the music like a pair of comfortable slippers. Beethoven had never flowed from my fingertips like this. I'd remixed his classical concerto with the hip-hop greats, and it was funky. Mozart was next, with a dash of Bach added for flavor and a touch of Pharrell for color.

"What's that, Reese? I've never heard The Greats like that before." Her hands were on her hips, and her smart shoes were tapping.

Yeah. This is hip-hop, baby. I cut my eyes at her. To my surprise, she was enjoying the flow. But only because she didn't know I'd mixed classical and hip-hop. If she'd known that, she would've had a straight fall-to-her-knees-and-wiggle-on-the-floor conniption fit. Immediately, I stopped playing, closed the lid on the ivories, and got up. "That's a piece I'm working on for Julliard," I lied, and then snatched up my knapsack. "I'll meet you at the school." *After I cop a new mixer to produce these beats*, I added in my head. I had a competition coming up, and I planned to win.

She wanted Julliard.

I wanted hip-hop.

May the best woman win.

ZIGGY PHILLIP

"I dance like no one's watching so everyone will."

Beep. Beep.

The cars blew by and their tires spit water from the pavement. On my left, I could see the street-cleaning truck barely moving as it washed the streets.

Beep. Beep.

"Hurry up, yo! Don't make me have to get out this car," some disgruntled driver was yelling at the car in front of him.

Looking at the fight I was sure was about to jump off, I stepped into the street without looking. Someone laid on their horn, then shouted at me. *Dumb move.*

"Yo. Yo. You better watch where you going!" A cabbie's head was out the window, yelling at me in the middle of traffic on One-two-five, One-hundred-twenty-fifth Street—Harlem, N.Y.

I banged on the hood of the yellow cab, a sight rarely seen up here. "'Yo,' back at you! Who you talking to like that? Man, this is a hundred-and-twenty-fifth street—Harlem—my playground. You better watch where you're going or take your butt back downtown where it's safe." I crossed in front of the car and waited in the middle of the street for the other morning traffic to pass. Who crossed at the corner anyway? Not me or the dozens of other people straddling the dotted white lines dividing one flow of vehicles from the other.

"Youngin'!" Sandman, the official unofficial mayor of Harlem, called from a milk crate he'd climbed on to preach to the passersby like he'd did every morning.

I waved. I didn't have time for Sandman this morning, but I needed to see what he wore. It had to be something from the sixties or seventies. He didn't rock today's gear, or any teeth.

"Youngin', I say. Come here." He was waving his hand, getting louder with each word. He stomped his dusty wing-tipped foot, and almost fell off of the crate.

I shook my head, laughing. I decided I'd go and give him some respect. He was the one who made stuff happen for me—for a price—like the vending license I'm too young to have.

"What's up, Sandman?" I asked, checking out his peach suit with purple pinstripes, and a blue flower in his lapel. Sure enough, his collar was long enough to reach his chest. No lie.

"Teaching. Preaching. And I tell you, youngin', don't let these streets eat you alive. In Harlem, only the strong survive. You better listen to what I say, I'm Sandman, the official unofficial mayor of Harlem. I don't play. These young girls walking these streets with strollers, snitching

on themselves about the beat they danced to nine months
ago with boys who aren't going *no*where. Watch 'em,
youngin'. They'll steal your dreams . . . and I'm not talking about the fast girls or the young daddies. I'm talking
about the babies. There's poison in their formula."

"Got'cha, Sandman. Thanks for the wisdom of the
day." I gripped my bag and walked away before he could
give me any more of his version of knowledge. I made it
to the other side of the street without a scratch or hiccup.
I had to go to school, but I also had to check on my vending table to make sure merchandise was stocked, and my
brother, Broke-Up, who had had more broken bones
than anyone I'd ever known, had singles for change.

"What 'appened, Z? Don't tell me you ah skip sk-ewl
dis marn-nin?" Broke-Up asked with a West Indian accent way thicker than mine. It was something he brought
back with him from Jamaica every year after spending
the summer there with our grandmother while I worked
slanging knockoff designer bags and bootleg CDs. "Dis
Sodom and Gomorrah!" he said, cutting his eyes at a guy
wearing skinny jeans, a fitted Alvin Ailey T-shirt, and a
pair of ballet slippers wrapped around his neck like jew-
elry. The dude was a dancer, a very good one I'd seen perform on many occasions. "You see that, Z?" Broke-Up
asked, sucked his teeth, and then spat. "Dis world sick.
Just sick. What kind of man walk around like dat? Him
no girl. What he wear tights pants for, not for de women.
Dat's why men should not dance."

I almost agreed with his nonsense like usual so I
wouldn't give myself away, but this girl caught my eye
with her thickness. I could only see her from the back,

but that was good enough. "English, Broke-Up. English. You're not on the island anymore."

"Yeah. Yeah. A'ight. But just so you know, I'm going to be selling my music. Cool?" he asked, switching back to his New York accent without a problem.

"Yeah. Cool," I answered him, my eyes still on the girl. "Psst, psst. Can I talk to you for a minute?" I asked her from behind. "Maybe buy you breakfast, beautiful?"

The girl looked over her shoulder and my stomach dropped.

Dang.

"Z, you're full of it. You already 'talked' to me," she bunny-eared her fingers and made air quotes. "Talked and talked and talked. Then you wouldn't call back."

I turned my head like I didn't see her. I didn't have time for shorty. But her sister . . . now *she* was a whole different story. She was Caribbean thick with Cooley hair, and the girl was smart. Now her—the sister—*she* could get it. Something serious. Any time of the day or night. I waved my hand in the air, telling the girl to push on. "So, Broke-Up, you got this, right? I'm not going to be able to pay attention in class if I have to worry about you and this table."

Broke-Up yawned, then laughed. "G'won, Z! I got this. You think I don't know how to hold down the vending table, eh? Let me break it down for you, Star. . . ."

I raised my eyebrows. No, I didn't think he could manage, but I didn't have a choice. I had to go to school. Had to get my Savion Glover and Alvin Ailey and Fred Astaire on so I could eventually choreograph videos and concerts for top-billing stars. Broke-Up, on the other hand, didn't have nothing to do, nowhere to go, and no dream to achieve. He also had no idea I was a dancer. No one in my family or on my block knew, and I was going to keep it like that. I was all male, I wouldn't give them the chance to question my sexuality or massacre my bravado. That's what they'd do if they had any idea, because where I came from, unless you were winding with some girl, you didn't dance. Dancing was for batty boys, homosexual men. And I sure wasn't one. I loved females. All of them, girls and women. But thick ones . . . yeah . . . they were my weakness.

"... and Coach bags are over here. One for fifty, two for eighty. And on this other side, we have the music. Remixes. Rap. R and B. Reggae. Calypso. Dancehall," he was still talking.

I pulled twenty-three singles out of my pocket, the only money to my name, and gave him eighteen. "You need singles to make change, Broke-Up. I'll catch you later." I was across the street, and headed to the train before he could stop talking. I had to get to school early so I could get a position up front. Mrs. Allen was the director and she didn't take no mess. She was also the one with the connects. And I needed to be connected ASAP, so I had to show her I was serious. Plus, I needed to see the selection of females that Harlem Academy had to offer. I crossed my fingers and asked Jah to bless me with some thick ones. Wasn't nothing like thick girls, good food, and dancing. And I was hungry for all three.

JAMAICA-KINCAID ELLISON

"I can act my way into and out of anything."

I sat in front of the tiny television with my eyes glued to the screen and my fingers crossed. Every day, the torment grew worse and upped my anxiety. How was I going to keep pulling this off? "By acting my way through it, of course," I said to myself, then finally exhaled when the morning news went off. I was so wrapped up in thinking that today was the day my picture was going to float across the screen with *missing* or *runaway* under it, that I hadn't even realize I'd been holding my breath. "Okay. This is it. The day of all days. The day my life changes," I pep-talked myself, and unfolded my body from its Indian-style cross-legged position on the floor.

My computer rang from the attached speakers, and my heart stopped. My hands started sweating and I could feel the flush rising to my hairline. I could do this. I knew this moment was coming, just as it had every first day of school for the last four years. Stepping over my pallet on the floor, I crossed the room to the makeshift table I'd assembled out of discarded milk crates that I'd borrowed from the store, then accepted the incoming call and sat in front of the screen. My mother's face blurred as it popped up on the screen. As usual, she was too close to the camera, and I knew without her speaking she'd be talking too loud. My parents were stuck in time, technophobes who could never get technology right. I smirked. If they weren't vegans, I'm sure they'd yell into drive-through speakers at fast-food restaurants.

"Good morning, Mother!" I greeted her, overly chipper. Being positive was a must-do in my family. There was no room for mediocrity of any kind, even if you felt that way.

"Good morning, Jamaica. Can you see me? Do you hear me?"

I could see the blur of her milky skin, and catch a glimpse of her always-perfect makeup and diamond earrings that were large enough to fund a small third-world country's hungry children for months, maybe years.

"Brad, honey. I don't think Jamaica can see me. I do believe it's time we have someone go to the school and set up audiovisual like on the set. . . ."

Hunh?! Panic started to roll in immediately. I didn't need audiovisual or them sending their people to make my space look like the Oprah Winfrey set; the same set my television-star dad had replicated because anything Oprah did had to be the best. My Mac was just fine, and

Skype was great. I didn't need anything for my dorm room because, though they had no idea, I wasn't tucked in it at the ritzy boarding school I'd been shuttled off to at eleven years old. I'd forged their signatures, all but emptied my bank accounts, paid my sister to keep quiet and rent me this nightmare of a studio apartment that I absolutely loved, then enrolled at Harlem Academy as soon as I'd been accepted.

"I can see you just fine, Mother. How's the beauty line coming?" I asked to throw her off topic and onto the one that was her favorite: her.

"The line is amazing. Did I tell you that we have stars wearing us now? We were mentioned at the Oscars. Great press . . ." She finally quieted, and I knew there was a problem. "Jamaica, is that a . . . *what* is that behind you? Your dorm room is hideous this year." She put her hand on the camera, trying to cover it, but I could still see her turn to my dad. "Brad, I think we need to go there and speak to someone. Jamaica's roughing it."

"Mother! Mother!" I shouted. "This is a temporary room that I'm studying in. The private study rooms are full," I lied.

"How about a study trailer, Jamaica? You know with the right attitude, environment, and belief, there's nothing you can't accomplish with a bit of hard work." My dad took his turn in front of the camera now. He wore his perpetual smile, and was in full motivational-guru mode.

"I'm fine, Dad. Really. I don't need a camera set, a study trailer, or anything. All I want is to go to school and be *normal* . . . and see you guys at Christmas, like always." I swept my blond dreadlocks from my face, and accidentally brushed the piercing under my lip, then rethought my normal statement. "I just want to be me. Okay?"

He clapped his hands together. "Christmas it is! But to make your mother feel better, we're going to wire money into your sister's account so she can help you purchase a car. She's eighteen now, so she can do it without us being there. We're going to computer-call her now. Love you, Jamaica. Over and out." The connection went dead.

I finally relaxed, knowing somehow and someway, I'd be able to pull off my charade for a few months without them knowing I'd moved to N.Y. and ditched their idea of prep school to prepare my way into the field of acting.

My stomach growled angrily. Without thought, I made my way to the barely a sneeze of a kitchenette and opened the refrigerator. Bare, except for the bottled water. I shrugged and opened a cabinet, and took out my last pack of sixty-cent cookies. They'd have to do because it was all I had, and I'd told myself to get used to it. I was "roughing it" as my mother had said, and I knew it wasn't going to change. They could deposit all the money into my sister's account that they wanted, but I knew I wouldn't see a dime of it. She'd keep it for payment to keep her mouth sealed. And I'd have to go out and try to find a job to support myself. But what could I do? I was the daughter of a supermodel mother and disgustingly rich motivational guru dad. I didn't know what it meant to be born with a silver spoon in my mouth. Our spoons were platinum. But to go to the Harlem Academy and breathe life into my dreams, I'd settle for plastic spoons with teeth at the ends.

Dreams were classless; it didn't matter what your socioeconomic background. And they were also colorless—I hoped. Because I knew for sure that in Harlem, I'd be the minority. The white girl with blond dreadlocks who would stop at nothing not only to thrive, but to belong.

FIRST SEMESTER

GET IN WHERE YOU FIT IN
TO
SHOW 'EM WHAT YOU'RE MADE OF!

1

LA-LA

Music pumped in the hallways like a party was taking place. Teens zigzagged through the maze of other students, most grouped together in cliques. Some were posted up against lockers watching rappers battle, and a group of break-dancers were rocking steady on a cardboard makeshift dance floor, all while the teachers and staff walked by, nodding their heads and encouraging what would be considered disorderly conduct at La-La's old school. She'd never seen anything like it in her life, and thought it was higher than tops. If she could've packed up her measly belongings and run away without her mother noticing some of her welfare check was missing—the part named La-La—she would've straight moved into Harlem Academy. It was that tight.

"Hey, pretty girl," some dude's voice carried over the dah-dump of music and chorus of teenaged voices competing to be heard in the crowded hall.

La-La looked to her left, saw some girl with the longest, curliest hair she'd ever seen framing the girl's pretty face. She was chewing a huge wad of gum, making it look delicious. She had full pouty lips, almond-shaped eyes, and OFF LIMITS stretched across her super huge ta-tas. La-La glanced down toward her floor-flat chest and saw straight to her Nikes, and knew why whoever-he-was was talking to the girl. She was beautiful and shapely, and La-La wasn't anything close.

The girl smiled and waved in La-La's direction. La-La didn't want her to think that she was all up in her business so she looked just past her, but could still see her in her peripheral.

"You," the girl said, pointing at La-La. "I'm talking to you. Yeah, you with the beautiful thick hair."

La-La snapped her attention the girl's way, then stuck her index finger to her chest. "Me?" She tried to smooth out her face because she knew it was twisted. Her expression was always the first thing to give her away, and she didn't want the girl to think she was nasty or rude, though she'd had a reputation for being that way at her last school. But who wouldn't after they'd been the target for bullies?

The girl waved again, then pushed herself off the locker she'd been leaning on. She was taller standing at her full height, and moved like an angel. The girl floated instead of walked, and made La-La feel even more stupid as she made her way over to her. "I'm Rikki, with two k's, and that boy over there, the one who keeps calling you 'pretty girl,' is my friend. I think he wants to talk to you. It must be the hair."

La-La's head spun and she almost died on the spot. The boy had not only called her pretty, but he was the same fine guy she'd seen in the admissions office weeks ago. Oh, she knew who he was all right. "Ziggy?" she asked just to ask.

Rikki looped her arm through La-La's and laughed. "Yeah. That's him. Ziggy. C'mon, I'll walk you over. You seem to be shy. I'm guessing it's 'cause you're new, but I know you're just fronting. You can't be shy, not if you're a student here. We perform and put on shows."

"Pretty girl, what's up?" Ziggy asked, then hugged La-La like they were old friends, and fingered her hair. "You and all this hair. It's fantastic."

After she inhaled his scent, she answered, but made sure to keep her lips as close together as possible to mask her teeth. "Thanks. Nothing's up. Just trying to maneuver around this place." She held out her schedule. "There's a blank here where my fifth class is supposed to be. I don't even know how I found the others. And I'm supposed to be meeting my sis, Cyd, for fifth period."

Ziggy and Rikki laughed. "That's supplemental time," he said, putting his arm around La-La. "That's for you to supplement your art."

She looked at Rikki for help because, clearly, she was the only slow one in the trio. "Girl, it's your free time. You can do whatever, just make sure you fill out a slip at the end of the month stating you've been honing your skills. We're artists around here, so they trust us to create. No babysitting at CAPA."

Ziggy nodded, then whistled at some thick-hipped girl walking by. "I gotta go, ladies. The thighs—" He paused, and figuratively morphed into a half insect, half animal. Licking his lips, he rubbed his palms together like a fly, then neighed like a horse. "I mean, lunch is calling." He left, running after the girl.

Rikki shook her head, smiling. "I forgot to add that other than him being my friend, he's also my patient."

La-La reared back her head, and swallowed the lump of jealousy lodged in her throat. "Patient?"

Rikki nodded. "Yep. He's got male-whore syndrome, and I'm trying to get him through it. But he's so charming and cute, and all the girls love him, so it's hard for him to help it. But it's only the thick girls I have to save him from. Ziggy loves him some big girls." She looked La-La up and down, then motioned at herself. "Girls like us, slim ones, don't stand a chance."

La-La's expression twisted into sour. "I heard that. Big girls need love too," she mimicked Big Boi's lyrics from an Outkast song. Then her eyes brightened.

"La-La!" Cyd waved, and then pushed her way through the students. She was rocking a funky fedora tilted just so on her head. La-La smiled. She hated hats, but Cyd made them look good. "What's up with fifth period? I can't find it." She made it over to them, holding out her schedule. "We do have the same class, right? At least, that's what I thought."

"No," Rikki answered for La-La, with her hand on her hip. She'd somehow changed in front of La-La's eyes, and slipped into an attitude.

Cyd looked Rikki up and down, and La-La could see a butt-kicking in Cyd's eyes. "Who are you?"

"I'm Rikki, since you want to know. La-La's new

friend. I'm also the one to tell you that you don't have a class fifth period. Because for fifth period we are scheduled to par-tay!" She broke out into laughter, and changed back into her cool self. "Got'cha!" She held out her hand to Cyd. "Couldn't resist. Sorry. But it's true. Funky hat, by the way."

La-La exhaled when she saw tension melt away from Cyd. "Oh, I was about to say. Whew!" Cyd made a production of wiping her forehead, then gave Rikki a pound. "Glad I didn't have to shake up lockers on my first day here. 'Cause I gets it in, ask La-La. I'm like an old-school scrapper."

All three girls laughed; then doom walked up.

Nakeeda.

La-La looked at her biggest hater on the planet, and her heart rammed in her chest. She'd known Nakeeda attended the school, but still wasn't prepared to see her. The girl had tormented La-La for the last three years, without reason, and had tried to turn everyone against her with fabricated material—i.e. lies—and had sent her a threat on a social networking site that she was going to beat her up on sight if she showed her face at CAPA.

"Didn't expect to see you here," Nakeeda hissed like the snake she was.

Cyd stepped forward, and literally walked in front of La-La. "You mean you didn't 'expect to see' anything, right? You're about as blind as you are dumb, and we all know your IQ falls into the negative. And why don't you get that chipped tooth fixed?"

Nakeeda placed her hand on her nonexistent hip. "This ain't about you, Cyd."

"Whoa. Whoa. Ladies. Ladies?" Rikki interjected, and shot La-La a questioning look. La-La shrugged.

"No, Nakeeda." Cyd said. "It ain't about *you*, that's the problem. You're mad—no, scratch that—you're jealous 'cause my girl got talent. Real talent. And you ain't got nothing but hustle. That's how you got in here."

Nakeeda scowled at La-La. "Oops. I never thought you two would admit it. 'Your girl,' hunh? I thought you twos were together-together."

Cyd lunged.

La-La grabbed her before she could reach Nakeeda and get expelled.

Rikki jumped in the middle. "What's going on?"

"Just because you handing out your body like fliers— to anyone who'll take it, and got a baby at fifteen—don't make the rest of us that way," Cyd spat, then turned to Rikki. "I'll tell you what's going on. Hoodrat here wants to torment La-La because La-La can sing, and No-Keeda here don't have no pitch, no range, and can only sing in one key. And she's still off in that key."

"Sing? Puh-leese. You call what La-La does singing? More like chirping." Nakeeda crossed her arms.

"Who's singing?" Ziggy appeared out of nowhere, asking. He pointed at Cyd.

Cyd pointed at La-La. "Word, pretty girl? Beautiful hair and you can sing?"

La-La pepped up. She couldn't help herself. It was something about Ziggy that moved her, and no matter if Nakeeda was there or not, she was going to shine as bright as she could to win Ziggy's attention. "More like *sang*; singing is for wannabes." She shot a glance Nakeeda's way. "I can blow a little sumthin'-sumthin'."

A beautiful smile parted Ziggy's lips, and his eyes shined. He lifted his eyebrows. "You know there's always a big competition coming up around here. We can schedule them ourselves. We didn't see the need because Nakeeda was already projected to be a winner, not enough competition—"

"Schedule one and I'm in. Say no more," La-La interjected, cutting him off, and swallowing her fear of the torment she knew Nakeeda was going to try inflict on her.

2

REESE

"An open audition at Bronx Science that can lead to Julliard," Reese opened her tangerine-glossed lips and the lie jumped out. A realistic tale she hadn't intended. It'd just spontaneously leapt from her mouth. And it was a good one.

A really good one that'll let me hook up with Blaze and work on the track, Reese praised herself, putting on a serious expression, and continuing to braid her blue-black locks with Native American hair-braiders. In the mirror, she watched her mother's reflection. Consideration painted Mrs. Allen's pretty face, and Reese knew she was finally free to fly the maximum-security co-op she'd been grounded to for the last two weeks. When she was busted for sneaking in at 1 A.M., her mother had caught her in a flat lie, called her father, then locked Reese down. Reese had fuzzed the truth, said she was going to the library to study for the pre SATs, and Mrs. Allen had shoved the dead alibi in Reese's face when she'd walked in. Reese hadn't been anywhere near where books were shelved, and her parents had seen to it that she wouldn't for a long time.

Her father, Mr. Missing in Action, finally joined her mother in the doorway. Stirring his cup of coffee, he stood silent. Turned into a human sponge. Sucked in the conversation as if he still really cared. But the truth was he didn't. He'd lost touch and was now trying to play catch-up while her mother took the charge he used to have. Just the sight of her dad made Reese's pulse percolate. She loved, hated, and missed him all at the same time. They'd been each other's favorites once, before he'd snatched away his attention from her, and BF'd her older sister, Montana. And became the enemy who handed down punishments via telephone, Skype, and emails. He'd made her mother the messenger, and Reese even more resentful. He hadn't the nerve or audacity to deliver news to Reese's face or ears. Could barely look her in the eyes. Most important, Reese believed, he hadn't the time for his youngest daughter. Not anymore.

Maybe never again. Reese rolled her eyes, then watched her parents from the mirror, pissed to the highest level. Their mandatory sentence was killing her groove, and they weren't being fair. Not in Reese's eyes. It wasn't as if she was a habitual liar. She only did what she had to do to get what she wanted, and didn't deserve to be cooped up. Especially because she hadn't told a complete lie—she just hadn't been completely honest. She had studied.

Hard. Had taken and received an almost perfect score on the pre SAT, and dominated the AP prep. As far as she was concerned, she should've been able to come and go as she pleased. At fourteen years old she could test out of just about any high school, and had had the chance to graduate from one of the hardest high schools to be accepted into. But, no, that wasn't good enough for her mom. Her mother wanted Reese to be a musician. And not just any music-playing genius; she had to be a classically trained one on a Julliard track.

"If I get picked, rehearsals'll start immediately," another lie ran out of her mouth, taking her conscience with it. Reese was on a mission and determined to do whatever to get out of the house—even betraying her parents. Lying to get what she wanted didn't bother her. Not anymore. And she wanted to work on a track and be with her boyfriend Blaze. Badly. Had to hook up with him during the day. Needed to make sure she didn't lose him or their sound. That's what she was most afraid of. Not being able to make the type of music she loved—hip-hop—and losing her boyfriend because her father had decided to step back in, fit *playing daddy* into his schedule, and ruin her relationship with the only other guy who cared about her. And Reese wasn't having it. She wasn't losing two guys she loved, and was convinced she could live with just having one, as long as it was him and the music.

"A *music* audition? At Bronx Science?" Mrs. Allen stood behind Reese, fixing the fringes on the bottom of Reese's braids while her father continued to listen. ". . . that requires you to dress like that? Come on, the crack of your butt is almost showing. And Bronx Science doesn't do music, Reese," she argued.

Reese turned, exasperated. Her stare landed on her seven-year-old nephew, Dakota, who had appeared out of nowhere, and he just smiled. Then she looked at her father, but he was unsurprisingly useless, and just shrugged. She turned her attention to her mother. The lady who would never get it. Anything outside of Harlem CAPA and Julliard were beyond her comprehension. And so was fashion. But not the arts. Her mom was right-brained, a creative soul who loved anything involving imagination. And Reese used it to her advantage. "*Mom.* It's not Science's production, it's just being held *at* Science. And Science does too do music. We're—well, I mean, since you separated me from my friends—*they're* more than mental calculators and scientific formulas, ya know? They have a theatre club. Call and ask. The play is like *Flashdance.* You gotta remember *Flashdance. . . .*" Reese breezed out of the bathroom with pep in her step because she was getting better at lying, and some organization really was holding auditions at the school. She'd checked the day before. Rushing ninety miles an hour to her room to get her things before her mother changed her mind, Reese turned up her lie. "It's like that. I *have* to stand out from my competition. That's why I have on my Native regalia," Reese yelled, slipping on knee-high moccasin boots.

Mrs. Allen followed. "Okay, but only because I support your dreams and creativity, and it'll look good on your music resume for college. But you know I don't like you running around with your butt showing. I deal with enough sex-crazed teenagers as it is. I won't have you being one of them," Mrs. Allen began.

"Ooh. Bad words!" Dakota reminded.

"Sorry, Dakota," Mrs. Allen apologized.

Reese tuned out the pair, then grabbed her backpack off the bedpost. She circled the too-pink bedroom, stuffing her must-haves into the purse. She sprayed on two mists of perfume, and tried to remember what she was forgetting. "Oh, lip gloss." She snapped her fingers, then found the flavored one Blaze liked.

Reese felt Mrs. Allen's stare on her back, and wished she'd ease up. Her mom was a former literary agent who'd represented erotica writers, and had made Reese's life torture because of it. She was scared Reese would indulge in the same thing that'd both made Mrs. Allen and her clients' beaucoup dollars once, and made her sister Montana a teen mother: sex. Reese didn't think it fair that she had to pay the price because of Mrs. Allen's past-career paranoia or be hung for her older sister Montana's mistake for getting knocked up young. No, Reese didn't think her mother was reasonable, even if she had entertained the thought once or twice. She was a teenager; she had all kinds of thoughts that would make her parents fall out and die if they could read her mind.

If only she knew. Reese gripped her bag, then headed toward the door.

"Meet me in the study before you go," He finally

spoke. That's what Reese had started to think of her dad as: He. A pronoun, not a father.

Reese stood in front of the desk her father never used, shouldered her bag, and placed her hand on her hip as she watched him sit. "Yeah?" was all she said. Four tiny contemptuous letters that echoed her anger.

"If it were up to me, you wouldn't go," He said. "I know you're lying."

But why isn't it up to you? she almost asked, then stopped herself. She knew if anyone could stop her, He could. Reese decided to plead the fifth, and not say a word. Not until she knew what her father was up to.

"The only reason I'm not interfering . . ."

Interfering? You're supposed to be my father, you idiot.

". . . is because I want your mom to be able to run things when I'm away—"

"Away?" Reese couldn't take it anymore. He'd only been home two days, and now He was off again? *He must have another woman. Another family, even. You stupid, dirty dog!* "What? You don't like us anymore? You just got here!"

For a second He hung his head.

Guilty, no doubt.

"I know, sweetie. But the record company has an issue that I need to take care of in the Cali division . . . and Montana has a medical conference there too. . . ."

"Sweetie?" *Now you're trying to patronize me.* "Montana? Oh. Yeah. I see." *Guess she's not mature enough to go to a conference by herself. She's only in med school to learn how to save lives. How dare she travel by plane? Alone.* "Sorry to disappoint you, Dad, but has it ever occurred to you to pick up the phone and call the school? Maybe, just maybe, this time I'm not lying. Maybe I'm just a teenage girl who's going to audition for a play you won't be able to see because you'll be in Cali. With Montana."

"And I'm going to need you to look after Dakota while I'm away. Your mother needs help."

I'm the one who needs help. Reese gripped her bag tighter and bounced out of the co-op just as her father began to dig deeper with his questioning. Before tears tracked down her face.

As soon as her feet connected with the pavement and moved toward the first thing rolling toward Central Park, Reese dialed Bronx Science to confirm her story would be backed up, then text-messaged Blaze, hoping he'd lift her spirits. She needed him more now than ever.

U MISS ME, MISS ME & STILL WANNA KISS ME? MEET ME @ R SPOT AS PLANNED. DON'T FORGET THE BEATS. GOTTA FINISH THE TRACK.

"Who knows, B? You're the only dude who seems to care about me now, so maybe I'll finally audition for you," she said to the picture of him she'd saved on her cell. Feeling better already, she puckered her lips and kissed the wind. Practiced for what she hoped would be a long evening, then quickly remembered that she couldn't pull it off alone. She might need backup to avoid her mom repossessing her Get Out of Jail Free card. And there was one person she knew would help. Had to. Her home girl and best friend, Wheez.

goin 2 meet b. may need u 2 cover 4 me. Reese blasted one last text message before going to hook up with her man to get her beats and kiss.

3

ZIGGY

Teachers, students, visitors, dancers, singers, actresses, musicians—all of the female persuasion—were tempting Ziggy as they made their way down the hallway. He didn't let one pass without scanning her with his X-ray vision—his pretend Superman power, but, still, for him and his vivid imagination it worked as if it were real, and he was sure he could see all of their underwear. Bikinis, thongs, little lacy racy numbers that climbed cheeks and inflicted wedgies, even granny panties, he believed he could see them all, and he loved them all. Even the grannies. He shook his head, walking on the tile with confidence. Tryouts for the major dance competition were only a few minutes away, and he was ready. He had to show the judges—the school, the world—that he had what it took to shine and, hopefully, ballet and hip-hop his way into a scholarship and a part of the prize money.

Harlem CAPA was expensive. He didn't know how much longer he could get Broke-Up to hold down his vending table while he went to school, and his tuition depended on the sale of bootleg designer purses and burned CDs.

His head turned left, then bounced right. He shook it in disbelief. Where did all these fine specimens come from? he wondered, barely able to walk straight. There was a sea of female pheromones drifting down the halls, and, happily, he was drowning in them. If only someone would look at him, give him a sign that they were interested so he could holler at them. As badly as he wanted to flirt, he was used to being prey.

Before he could pick one girl from the crowd that he had to have, someone snatched him inside a doorway and slammed him against the wall, his back bouncing off of it with a loud thud. Like a flash, his assailant was all over him, covering his eyes with a hand. Though he couldn't see, relief swooped through him. A dainty hand, all soft and warm, made him feel better. Figuring out his attacker was female made his heart dance instead of race. But who was she? Pulling the soft palm away from his skin, he still couldn't make her out. She was too close and swift, and the vestibule was too dark. He hadn't seen her coming, and really didn't care from where she'd come. All he knew was that she was there, holding him hostage, and planting kisses on his cheeks and forehead like he was a baby, and she kept mumbling something that sounded sweet.

She'd appeared out of nowhere like a ghost, but she

sure didn't smell like one, he discovered. Her aroma was delicious.

Ah . . . he thought, that's how he'd be able to tell who she was. Her scent. Inhaling deeply, he drew the sweetness into his lungs. *Vanilla-honey like pretty-girl Chance from one hundred thirty-eighth? No. Maybe it's the softness of jasmine I smelled on La-La, the thin baby-face girl with the sultry voice? No. Or is it lavender like Moni, the bohemian-looking sista with the power to relax people like her scent? No again.* Ziggy shook his head. The girl didn't smell like any of the girls in his mental Rolodex. He shut his eyes tighter, hoping one turned-off sense would heighten another, and he'd be able to sniff his way to an answer. He had to because heaven and earth forbid he call out the wrong name. The last time he'd done that, he'd limped for two days, lost a girlfriend and a dance competition because he couldn't compete due to crazy-girl-inflicted injuries.

"What, you forgot me already?" the unknown girl mumbled in his ear, still planting kisses from his forehead to his chin.

Ziggy decided to play dirty. He cocked his head to the side, almost sure he could place the voice. If only he could get her to speak again. "Wow. You that forgettable? That's too bad."

A hand pushed back his head, murking him. "Shuddup, Z. You ain't nevva gonna be able to forget me . . . not after this summer."

There. He had her. He reared back his head, peeked a little, and was blinded by a chipped tooth. "Nakeeda!?"

He stomped his foot, and pushed past her. "Nakeeda!? *Ill.* Are you crazy?"

"You ain't think I was crazy weeks ago," she reminded him, making his stomach turn. "You was all over me like heat in the summertime. Wait—it *was* hot and summertime."

"Ooh," someone said, then crashed to the floor sounding like a bag of bricks.

Ziggy took that as his cue to walk, jumping back like the sound scared him. But it only took one look for him to switch from fear to laughter. A glance at the sneaker, scuffed on the toe with black marks, told him who'd taken the spill. "Half-Dead? That you . . . again?"

Half-Dead turned his face toward Ziggy and cursed. "Can you believe somebody tripped me?" he asked, fumbling the truth.

"Yeah, you tripped you. You were dancing again, hunh?" Ziggy held his stomach in laughter, one finger pointing toward Half-Dead on the floor.

Nakeeda made her appearance, stepping out of the recessed doorway. "Half-Dead, you do know your foot's dead, right?" she pointed out, then crossed her arms under her breasts.

"Shuddup, chip-tooth. My whole foot ain't dead. Just half of it. My toes." He looked at Ziggy with a what-were-you-doing-with-her look. "I know y'all ain't together. Can't be that bad out here, playa."

"You shuddup, dead foot! I'm a catch!" Nakeeda declared.

Half-Dead managed to get up from the floor. He

hopped on his good foot. "Yeah, you a catch, all right. Somebody gone mess around and catch something from you."

Ziggy laughed again.

"You ain't with her right, Z?"

Ziggy shook as if he were a dog shaking water off his fur. The thought of him and Nakeeda got under his skin, and he'd blamed the summer mistake on heat exhaustion, lack of sleep, and that tiny bathing suit she'd worn that had left nothing to the imagination. "Nope! I gotta go. I'll see y'all around." He walked away, ignoring her threats and insults.

"Z! Z! Over here," another familiar voice called.

Ziggy followed the voice. "Rikki! The only love of my life who I don't love like that, what's up?" he asked, pushing his way through the crowded hallway until he reached her, glad to be free of Nakeeda, that chipped tooth, and the fastness that made her too easy for him to want. In one quick reach, he pulled Rikki into a bear hug and swung her around. "Where've you been? I was calling you, knocking on your window to see if I could crash at your crib after the dance-offs today. You know, basically trying to track you down. But no Rikki." He shook his head, and released her from his brotherly hug. "What, you finally found you someone worthy or something? You cakin' and boo-loving, Slick Rik?" he teased.

Rikki swept her long curls from her face and smiled. "That's you, player-player. I'm not into all that. So you ready for the competition?" she asked.

Ziggy held a finger to his mouth, looked around for

Nakeeda, then nodded. Was he ready? He was more than prepared for the tryouts and the girl he knew was in there waiting on him, but just didn't know it yet. "Let's be clear, there is no competition. I am *the* man. And let's not forget, these are the auditions for the auditions."

It was Rikki's turn to laugh. "Right, I forgot. You have to try out just to be able to make the real tryouts." She stuck her finger into his chest. "And yes, you're the man a'ight. The man who's hiding his ballet slippers!"

Ziggy snatched Rikki by her arm, pulling her down the hallway. "Shoes, Rik. Shoes. Slippers are for fairies. I rock Timbs and sneakers—and audiences and girls, when I perform."

"And obviously a clouded perspective like your family. *'Fairies,'* really? We talk like that now?" She pushed open the door to the room where the competition was being held.

And there she was. *Her.* Ziggy's eyes bulged at the love of his life, whom he'd been admiring since a year ago when he'd spotted her at another competition. "Dang, Rik. You see her? I gotta have her," he proclaimed, meaning every word. He'd never been affected by a girl the way he was now.

Rikki rolled her eyes.

Beautiful and alone. Ziggy admired her from behind. Fresh twists. Greased scalp gleaming under the bright lights. A body to die for, be resurrected for, and drop dead for again. Immediately, he dropped his bag, seeing a chance to dance his way into her life. She clearly needed a partner, and he was just the one. As if the gods were smiling down on him, the track she grooved to switched from fast R & B to a hip-hop reggae mix, both his specialties. With a sly smile on his face, he looked over at Rikki, and winked. Before this song came on he'd known he had the ability to get her attention, but with the island-infused hip-hop beat, he was certain he could rock her and hold it. In seconds, he was feet from her, and he only broke his groove to fan himself from the heat. Just looking at the girl had made him warm. Caused him to lose concentration. He kicked off his shoes and closed his eyes, and focused on the hardwood under his bare feet. He'd gotten lost in the music again, and mentally traveled back in time to Jamaica, where he'd learned and perfected a very masculine version of the Dutty Wine.

"You can do it, Z! Dance. Show dem gals there how we do," his brother's words rang loud within. He opened his eyes, the words drowning out any hesitation he'd had about tantalizing the fine specimen in front of him and making him cut loose. This type of dancing his family wouldn't object to. He could wind all day, and they wouldn't question his manhood or sexual preference. A smile tugged at the corners of his mouth as he worked his way behind the girl, and grabbed her hips. Normally, he'd have been too forward, disrespectful even. But not today, not with her. She was too good for his normal tactics.

"Allow me," Ziggy whispered in her ear when he felt her stiffen. "Relax, sweet girl, it's only a dance." Quickly he spun her, pulled her into him, then arched her backward, sweeping her long braids back and forth on the studio floor. In an upside-down U, she became his puppet, and he worked her magic better than many professional conga dancers. He got extremely low with it, repeatedly made her shoulder blades touch the floorboards like he'd learned watching couples dance on TV.

Touch. Lift. Touch. Lift. Touch. Hold. Caress. He repeatedly ordered the girl's shoulder blades, his body no longer dancing with hers on the hardwood but making a love connection. Sexily, he swayed her curved form to the music as the girl shook her bosom and tastefully thrust her hips. He unfolded her into a stance, their faces close enough to inhale each other's breath. Immediately, he released his weight to the ground, dropping to his knees in front of her, and then prowled tigerlike on all fours while his pelvis gyrated in sync with the heavy drums. Sweat formed on his brow as he danced harder, and tried to outdo the other dancers who'd begun to spill into the audition room. He was competitive. Used to being the best. He loved attention, and now wanted to captivate not only the fine girl, but the instructor he'd noticed walking in. The girl locked eyes with him, lending him her energy. Her smile was megawatt, and her body was flexible, Ziggy noticed as he took her in one last time before closing his eyes. Later he could daydream about her, maybe even talk to her. But it was showtime now, and he had to focus.

"You two," the instructor said, slicing Ziggy's flow. He pointed at Ziggy and the girl. "You're partners."

Ziggy tilted his head. "I thought this was a singles' competition."

The instructor, resembling more of a scientist than a dancer, scratched her head. "It is, but there's also a couples'. If you don't want to be a part of it . . ."

"Oh, count us in; we're a part of it. We're in." Ziggy looked at the girl, smiling. Now he had three competitions to look forward to. The singles. The couples. And the biggest one of them all—getting the girl.

4

JAMAICA-KINCAID

Her phone vibrated before she reached the corner where she was supposed to turn. Jamaica moved her locks out of her face, adjusted her wire-rimmed sunglasses, and stopped walking. She'd been waiting to hear from Gully, her old dorm mate, about an upcoming audition that Gully couldn't make. She whipped the phone out of the case, read Gully's text, and smiled. Jamaica didn't know how she'd pulled it off, but she had. After only days in Harlem, Jamaica already had her first shot at a real acting gig. A teensy part but, still, a chance.

"You *lost*?" a guy's voice asked from behind.

Jamaica turned, looked up, and grinned at the fine man-child towering at least a foot and a half above her. Dark hair, emerald-green eyes, and deep copper skin gave away his Spanish heritage. He was gorgeous. And she guessed his male beauty wasn't only skin deep because his face wore a look of concern, told her that he was car-

ing and not just good looking. She didn't know why she
was smiling at him, because he hadn't a hint of a grin. He
was just so cute, and there was something welcoming
about his expression.

"I don't think so." She pulled her schedule from her
pocket, and glanced at the school's address.

Now he smiled. "Let me *see* that." He reached for the
paper, then read it. "*Oh*, you're here already. It's just
around a couple corners. I'm going the same way. *Follow*
me."

Jamaica nodded, then did as he instructed. "So you go
to CAPA too?"

He nodded. "Yep, *and* believe it or not, I also *go* to
your apartment building."

Jamaica froze. She'd heard many things about New
York, not all of them good, and now she worried. How
did he know where she lived?

"We're *neighbors*," he explained, stopping next to her.
"Don't worry, I'm not one of the *crazies*. I live across the
hall from you. I left right after you this morning, then we
were in the train station together. I'm surprised you didn't
see me." He laughed. "You know you *really* need to be
more observant. There aren't too many people who look
like you in the neighborhood." He offered her his hand.
"I'm Mateo."

Jamaica introduced herself, feeling even better than she
had seconds ago. It wasn't because he was super cute. She
wasn't attracted to him like that, and he didn't seem to be
interested in her either. It was his vibe. He was just cool
in an intoxicating wanna-hang-around-him way. Plus it
was nice to meet someone who went to the same school,

and shared a neighborhood. Now she didn't feel so alone.

"So what's *your* art?" he asked, after they'd resumed walking, and turned the corner.

"I'm an actress. You?"

He smiled, then shrugged. "Let's just say I'm a *late* bloomer. I'm pretty good at most arts: music, singing, dancing, etcetera, etcetera. They want me to act or sing, but I don't know *what* I want to do yet." He pulled open the heavy metal school door and held it open for her. "So you wanna eat together at lunch? I can introduce you to some people. This is my second year here, and I'm pretty *pop*ular 'cause, ya know, my extraordinary personality is just *so* magnetic that no one can resist," he teased.

Jamaica shrugged and raised her brows. "Depends on what you're doing later. Say, around three?"

Mateo mimicked her, shrugging his shoulders and raising his brows too. "*Whatever.* As long as we keep brow lifting *and* shrugging, count me in!"

She laughed, not only at his joke, but at the fact that he stressed at least one word in everything he said. It was hilarious and such a contrast to his handsomeness. "Deal. Well, since your personality is *so* extraordinary *and* magnetic, I could use company on the way to this audition I have. Maybe some of your magnetism can rub off on me before we get there, and then they won't be able to resist my acting skills."

"You call that acting? Can you *act* like you can *act*?"

Great, another guy inflecting words. Jamaica almost fainted from anger. She couldn't believe this mess of a man in front of her berating her talents. But he was the genius in charge, and she was desperate. But, if she could've slapped him with the director's chair and still gotten what she'd wanted, she would've hit him with the piece of furniture twice. Hard. Shattered his face, his ego, and his pride like he was doing to her confidence. But she wasn't even close to violent, and she couldn't knock him down even if she really wanted, so she swallowed her anger and crossed her tanned legs. She repositioned herself in the uncomfortable seat. Settling back, she cut her eyes low, looked up at Maritzio, the Italian director who was a gift to the American movies. The latest hotshot, he commanded top pay and the best actors. He also liked new blood.

Jamaica rotated her ankle, and ordered her hands not to wring one another or his neck. Nervous wasn't the word for the shaken energy moving through her or the anger firing up her pulse. If she proved herself, impressing Maritzio with the talents she knew were hiding deep within but didn't seem to want to surface, her opportunities would shuttle to the heavens. If he continued to ridicule her with his uncensored slights, any chance she had would be dead because she'd shuttle him across the room, face-first into the wall. She was there for an acting gig, a chance to be glimpsed so she could eventually be watched. Gully had been nice enough to offer her the chance to audition for the super-small part, but a Hollywood acting career was what she really wanted—what she'd always dreamed. She had to have a chance to show and capture a big-screen audience with her acting abilities, not bore it with a second-rate B part. Extra parts were easy, and the few lines she was auditioning for weren't too far above extra. Something anyone could do. But Jamaica had something else. A special talent. She could cry on cue, totally suspend the audience's disbelief in seconds like Aristotle wrote about in his *Poetics*, and she'd promised herself that she'd make history. But first she had to win this uppity Maritzio over so he could introduce her to the masses as the star she was destined to be.

"Focus. I need you to blossom, not close up," he snapped. Literally snapped his fingers at her like she was some lowly waitress taking too long to serve him.

Jamaica nodded. They'd been through this twice already because he knew she had *it* because he'd glimpsed *it*. That's what he'd told her, and she wanted to believe him. If only she could find *it* again, she'd certainly give *it* to him. Nervously, she uncrossed her legs, then lifted her five-foot body from the chair. In a pair of hot-pink shoes, flesh-tone pants, and ratty faux-fur coat, she strode back to the X marking her spot in stage center, and felt the heat of the lights and pressure.

Maritzio gave her the action sign, letting her know it was her turn to give him *it*. Jamaica shivered, crossed her arms over her chest, and prominently stuck out her foot like she'd been instructed. "I'm hungry, mister. Please help. You can have my shoes for a dollar," she said, hoping she'd delivered her three lines to satisfaction. Maritzio's lips turned up into a smile. Well, his version of a grin.

"Great. Great," Maritzio praised. It was the way he'd dismissed all the other actors, that's what Jamaica had heard from a few of the ones who had graced the stage before her. And she trusted their words when he set his clipboard on the table next to him. "*Finito*!"

Jamaica walked over to him and shook his hand, thanking him for the opportunity. "Thank you," she said again, still holding his hand, trying to convince him that she was nice and liked him.

He shook his head and waved away the thanks. "My pleasure, young lady. You're a very talented girl. When you understand that, you'll become it a thousand times over."

Jamaica smiled, happy for it all to be over, then walked away chastising herself. *Why'd I have to be so eager and shake his hand?*

The sun spilled its lemon light on the Spanish Harlem neighborhood as cars hustled on both sides of One Hundred Tenth Street. Taxi horns blared at other cabs; drivers yelled at other cabbies to pick up their passengers and move out of their way or get off the street. Kids crossed the wide, busy lanes with slices of pizza, ice cream, and beef patties with cheese. And a Dominican food truck, parked on the corner, provided shade for the teenage boys who shot a game of Cee-lo, all hoping for the four-five-six that'd make them win the pot while someone pushed a cart of frozen ice in tropical flavors. Jamaica surveyed her surroundings and wondered how long she'd be safe. She liked the people, the Spanish music that blared until all times of the night, and the safety that the thugs in the unsafe area provided. If you were in with the ruthless, the bad didn't come after you—that's what

Mateo told her. So she was determined to learn the ways and people in her neighborhood. Still, though, she was tempted to pack up and move to Greenwich Village, an artsy and eclectic part of Manhattan where she believed an actor of her talents should bunk, and utilize money her parents could easily send her if she came up with the right lie. But that'd be too hard, especially with her sister receiving her funds. Plus, that would be caving. She had to make it on her own with talent.

"Don't feel bad, Jamaica," Mateo said, pulling her toward him in a side hug. "This is New York, there's *always* opportunities."

She forced a smile on her face, then nodded. "I guess you're right. Wanna come by my house for Ramen noodles and cold faucet water? I boiled it last night, so it's cleaner than tap."

Mateo laughed. "*Ramen* noodles? *Wow*!" He playfully swatted her locks, then swept her outfit with his eyes. "You're rocking *five*-hundred-dollar jeans. That shirt cost at *least* a buck, and I don't even want to guess how much the shoes cost, but last I checked he doesn't make a pair under *four*. What, you *never* heard of a consignment store, or something? I thought girls who looked like *you* ate better."

Jamaica rolled her eyes. "Girls like me have to eat Ramen noodles until we find jobs. My parents used to buy my clothes, but now I have to support myself, Mateo. And I didn't bring enough clothes with me to even think about consigning any."

"Aren't you an actress, like theater *and* movies?"

Jamaica nodded. "Sure. I can do any type of acting.

And I'd love to work in theater one day. You kind of have to to show you're a serious actor—and definitely for under pay scale, too."

"Well, if that's the case I give you a definite *no thanks* to the Ramen noodles. I'll pass. But you can come by *my* crib for dinner. My mom's making *el pollo guisado*—Spanish for stewed chicken."

She nodded, still smiling. This time genuine.

"*And* maybe . . ."

Jamaica bit. "Maybe what?"

"Maybe *you* can talk to my moms. She works for a *couple* of theater people."

5

LA-LA

Her hands twisted and sweated as she wrung them nervously. She knew she could do it, had done it before, but only alone and in front of strangers. Rikki, Ziggy, and Cyd stood feet in front of her, two steps ahead of the rest of the dance class, with their focus on her. Every time they inhaled, she felt as if they were stealing her breath. The huge room with slick wood floors, mirrors that stretched from her feet to the ceiling, and waist-high ballet bars seemed to close in on her.

"You gonna sing or not?" That was Cyd, slapping her hand on her curvaceous hip.

Ziggy's eyes left La-La and moved to Cyd. "Stoppit, gal, you gonna make me"—he bit his lip and growled playfully—"eat you up up in here."

La-La looked at Rikki, pleading in her eyes, and nodded toward Ziggy.

You like him? Rikki mouthed.

La-La shrugged.

Rikki rolled her eyes. "Another one bites the dust," she whispered, smiling. She stretched her neck toward Ziggy. "Z, you gotta go! Conflict of interest. Aren't you judging the competition?"

Ziggy threw up his hands, then began to dance. He bounced, buckling down to his knees; then he swept them across the floor in a square pattern, finally picking himself up one leg at a time. He began locking, then gyrating. La-La was sure she was going to die from internal combustion. The movements of his body and the expression on his face were scrumptious. There was only one way he'd be able to move like that, she surmised. Ziggy had had a lot of practice dancing with girls, and not on a dance floor.

"Okay. Okay. You're right as usual, Rikki. But you can't blame me for wanting to see a pretty girl sing. I'll be rooting for you La-La," he said as he moonwalked his way out the double doors.

The classroom full of dancers mumbled their dislike for waiting.

"This is a performing arts school, so perform already," a boy called out.

"What? You need music or something?" asked a girl who looked like she was running for The Girl Next Door/Plain Jane award.

"Why? You gonna beat box it or something, prep girl?" ever-protective Cyd asked.

The girl stepped forward, walked over to the piano

stationed in front of the room, and took her place on the bench.

"Really?" Rikki said. "What're you gonna play, Reese? Beethoven?"

"Hum a little so I can pick up your BPMs," the girl named Reese instructed.

Cyd, La-La, and Rikki looked at her with raised brows.

"Beats per minute. You know, speed?" Reese asked.

With a body less than ninety-pounds, La-La opened her mouth, and hummed loudly, as if her lungs alone weighed more than she did. The room quieted and Reese, the plain girl, made love to the piano with her fingers, tickling it until it sung. La-La closed her eyes, and let the music lead her; then she snatched the reigns, and led it where she wanted it to go. Tears streaked from her cheekbones to her chin, then dropped to her shirt. The music was lovely, so, so lovely, that she couldn't help cry. Before she could finish the song, the room erupted with clapping, stomping, and a loud rumble she couldn't recognize.

"Encore!" the boy who had dared her to perform yelled before she was done.

Hands wrapped around her, pulling her tight. Then another pair embraced her. La-La opened her eyes, then smiled. Rikki was to her left, Cyd to her right and, somehow, Ziggy had made his way back into the room. He stood in front of her, nibbling his lip, and telling her he wanted her with his eyes.

"You should let me take you out," he said, and changed her whole world.

*   *   *

Even though it was a rainy day, Times Square subway was filled to capacity, as La-La knew it would be. She'd sung at the school with great reception, but she needed a *Showtime at the Apollo* audience, and knew New Yorkers who rode the train would give her just that. If she was good, they'd let her sing. If she didn't cut it, they'd cut her off, and then tell her to go home without apology or hesitation. She shrugged her shoulders, pulled her wet shirt from her skin, and decided the show must go on. Thunder roared from above over the loud rumble of the trains moving in and out of the station.

"You gonna sing looking like that?" Cyd asked, reaching for La-La's roots. "I mean natural hair is cute and all, but it's not so sexy once it's rained on."

La-La's eyes bulged as she touched her hair. "Oh, no. I don't want to look completely homeless. It's bad enough these people are probably thinking I'm a bum for singing in the train station."

Cyd took off her fedora and placed it on La-La's head. "And the difference between singing *on* the train and singing *in* the train station is . . . what?"

La-La smiled. "On the train, I can just jump off at the next stop. But I guess you're right." She zigzagged through the crowd, finding a spot a few feet from a drunk who'd taken up residence on the dirty ground. "Here goes," she said, alerting Cyd.

Cyd pressed play on the CD player, and an instrumental began to play. "Old-timer's music? Really? You are so old-school, La-La."

La-La shot Cyd a work-with-me look. "I'm singing Marsha Ambrosius, Raheem DeVaughn, then Melanie Fiona if they don't boo me out of here." She adjusted her borrowed hat, then began to belt out lyrics. Totally into the song, La-La managed to smile with her mouth open. The train riders were snapping their fingers, humming along, and some began to gather in an arc in front of her. Throwing up her hands, she somehow grazed her earring, making it fall to the ground. Immediately she bent to pick it up, never stopping her flow. The fedora fell topside down, and she went to reach for that too, but someone dropped coins into it, then someone else dollars.

"Keep singing," Cyd said, pulling La-La into full stance. "They're paying you, girl. Paying you!" She began to cabbage patch dance while guarding the hat and La-La's money. "This is my girl, right here! My girl. Next stop, *Billboard* magazine and Madison Square Garden!"

La-La felt so light and heady that the subway stairs felt cotton-soft under her feet as she and Cyd ran out of the subway station. As many times as she'd sung on the train, she'd never been paid to do it. Finally, she felt free, as if her voice could really take her somewhere. And she also felt something else, too. That the orthodontist was near. She was on top of the world, and if she had anything to do with it—which she did—she was going to have Ziggy with her.

In mid-stride, she grabbed Cyd's arm, stopping her.

"What?"

La-La smiled. "Can I use your cell phone? I want to

call Ziggy, see if his offer to take me out is still good? If he was serious," she threw into the air.

Cyd looked at her, crossing her eyes. "Duh. Of course, he was serious. Did you see what he was wearing?"

La-La crinkled her eyebrows. "Sweats, I think?"

Cyd elbowed her, handing her the phone. "Yeah. Sweats topped off by lust!"

6

REESE

Reese rubbed her bare arms, warming herself as a cool wind swept in from the nearby lake, chilling her and Blaze's meeting place: a shaded recess in Central Park where they'd cuddle and talk without interruption. But Reese knew when she checked her watch, there would be no hugging or kissing today, just like the last time she'd texted Blaze to meet her. She walked out into the sunshine and the unusually desolated park. The emptiness was vast and eerie, magnified by the clearness of the daylight. There were no snotty-nosed toddlers accompanied by bored-looking nannies in sight. Not a jogger or bicyclist or roller-blader whizzed by. More importantly, Reese huffed, there was no Blaze. Again. Her boyfriend was forty-nine minutes late when she needed him the most, and Reese felt alone. And angry. She'd been disappointed by the two guys in her life in too short of a time span. Her father, she couldn't curse out. But she could let

Blaze have it, she decided as she went to go find him to give him a verbal whipping. She'd given him one pass when he flaked out last time and didn't return her text message when she had Wheez covering for her; now he was standing her up again. Never mind the kiss she'd entertained giving him, she needed the 808 drums for the track she was working on. And he was the only person she knew who had that drum machine, the only one that gave the eardrum-rattling hardcore baseline she needed.

Reese stomped to West Fourth Street Courts, then paused in front of the enclosed basketball square known as The Cage. Lacing her fingers through the building-high, chain-linked fence that separated the boys' playground from the sidewalk, she inhaled deeply. Literally sniffed out her man. His view was blocked by hoopers and onlookers, but he was definitely nearby. The unmistakable scent he wore like cheap cologne alerted her. Sweet. Tangy. Funky with a capital F, the pungent aroma snitched his whereabouts, and turned her stomach. And so did the 'heads who'd surrounded him to buy his novice-scientist-invented "healthy" green that perfumed the air with its stench.

Excusing her way through the crowd, Reese inched up on him. Shaking her head and rolling her eyes, she fumed anger. Not only had Blaze stood her up for their Central Park hookup again, he'd lied to her. "Uh-uhm," she cleared her throat to gain his attention.

Blaze didn't look up. Just sat with his head hanging, clearly focused on the knot of money he was sorting by denomination. "What's gonna make you better?" he asked, inquiring about how much she wanted to buy, not her health.

Reese exhaled. Her anger fueled by hurt. "Ripping you a new one, that's what'll make me feel better!" she hissed.

With head still down, Blaze lifted his bloodshot eyes to meet her glare. For seconds they held their stares; then he laughed. Chuckled. Fell back in tears. Giggled like a toddler being tickled. "Yo, Reese. Stop it. I never said I was retiring from the game, I *said* I was taking a vacation," he explained, raising up two fingers in the air. "My two weeks are up."

Reese shook her head so hard she was sure it was going to fall off. Blaze was as high as his customers. "No, B. You promised you'd stop. What, you wanna get kicked out of UCLA's chem program before you get accepted? Bad enough you smoke like fire, you gotta spread it too?"

Blaze doubled over in laughter, then toked on the toxic stuff wrapped in cigar paper. He blew the smoke in Reese's face, and it sickened her more. "Ha! See Reese, even you know this good-good is *fire*. And you don't smoke. Well, these people do," he pointed out, slicing his hand through the air at the surrounding crowd. "They need it, remember? Well, I got it. Economics, baby. If I don't supply their demand, they'll be sick."

"*Sick?* You must've hit that one too many times. You're crazy," she accused, tossing back her hair and accidentally inhaling the scent. Immediately, her head felt lighter, and she worried. Drugs were disgusting and a turn-off. "You don't do this for medicinal purposes, B. These are 'heads, not patients."

"True. True," he agreed, nodding. "But at least I sell 'em the good-good. *Organic*, remember? Not chemically enhanced like the garbage they're used to. So in a way, I'm preventing them from possibly developing a disease, and making 'em feel good at the same time."

"Handle your business then, Dr. Feel Good," Reese huffed, turned her back to Blaze, and patted her butt. *And you can kiss this while you're at it.* "I'm going to the school to see if I can sneak into the music studio. I'll find a way to make a hard bass line myself."

Tears threatened to roll as Reese pushed her way back through the crowd headed toward the 2 train. She'd had enough of Blaze's nonsense. His ridiculous idea that organic green does a body good, and that he'd clearly chosen the 'heads over her. She was tired of coming in second, and had to find a way to move to the top of his and her dad's VIP lists. True, what she'd had planned for Blaze wouldn't have fattened his pockets as much as his activities, but, in time, she was sure they could have made a lot of money together with hit records. But the lure of a hot music-industry future together didn't seem to be enough to stop Blaze from dealing.

Reese wiped away her tears before they fell. "Your loss, B," she whispered, boarding the train. "Today was going to be our day," she said, sinking down onto the first available seat she'd spotted, feeling as empty as it'd been before she filled it. She fingered the iPod in her pocket, hating that she'd fallen for a wasted talent. She and Blaze were a dynamic duo in the studio, capable of making monster hits, and he was tossing everything important to the wind for nonsense. The music and her. She knew then what she had to do: She'd give him one more chance, and if he didn't step up and stop his dealing, she'd just have to find someone else who could bang a track like he did. She wasn't ready yet to be alone.

The One hundred twenty-fifth Street train station was more crowded than usual, Reese thought as she pushed through the people and up the stairs to the street. Before she planted both feet on the sidewalk, a sound louder than the music blasting in her ears through her headphones made her pull them out. She stopped. Paused. Looked both ways on the always busy street, and almost choked. The heaviest bass she'd ever heard had stolen her breath and was now taking over her body. "Dang," she finally said, able to speak but not move, at least not toward Harlem CAPA. She had to follow the music.

"Don't!" An older man with a shock of gray hair held out his hand, stopping her. He loomed tall over her, and wore a three-piece wool suit that was obviously too hot for the weather. Upon closer inspection, Reese saw the suit was a dirty olive green with tiny pink polka dots, and had an orange and gold pinstriped lining.

"Don't what?" Reese asked, easing around the man and the crate he stood on.

"Don't push me . . ." he began, singing the Grandmaster Flash song; then he stopped abruptly. "Reese, aren't you supposed to be in school?"

Hunh? "How do you know my name?" she asked, really ready to kick up dust and get away from him.

"I'm Sandman. I know everything. Ask around, little

lady. And if you ever need something, the sun, moon, or stars . . . come to me. I can get it for you—for a price. And be careful. These streets will eat you up."

Reese walked away shaking her head. There were all types in New York, but Harlem had some real specialties, she thought, moving toward the vendor with the hypnotic beats.

"What 'appened, pretty gal. You want a Coach bag, Gucci . . . ? 'Ow 'bout music? Sandman sent you here?" a young familiar-looking Jamaican guy asked her before she made it to the front of the vending table.

"No. That man's crazy. What's that song? Whose is it?" Reese asked, moving her head back and forth like a turkey like she was in the studio. She was vibing. Hard.

"He don't mean no harm. He just looks out for everyone on the street. He's like a historical landmark around here. He used to be famous or something. But anyway, you a producer, gal? Moving your 'ead like that?"

Reese smiled. She'd never heard herself called a producer before, and loved the ring of it. "Yes. Name's Reese. And I need some drums like that. And that bass is killing it. Whew!" she banged on the table, her fists keeping tune to the bass line. "Killing it!"

The guy smiled. "Broke-Up's my name, and that track be my game. I made that, pretty gal. I makes tracks like that in my sleep. Easy."

Reese cocked her head to the side. "Really?"

Broke-Up laughed, and a customer approached the table and took his attention. Reese didn't know whether to believe him or not. His actions told her he wasn't serious, so she walked off to see if she could sneak into Harlem CAPA. She had beats to make, not time to waste on cute Jamaican boys who pretended to make hot tracks. She already had two great pretenders in her life; she didn't need one more.

7

ZIGGY

Work it. Work it! he pushed himself, lifting his body off the floor. *Could'a did that move better,* his inner critic chastised. Sweat dripped now, flew from his glistening brown skin as he rolled his head side to side, then whipped it in a circle. Ziggy flung his arms wildly, yet smoothly, making a difficult African fertility number seem easy. The bottoms of his feet caught fire from stomping and jumping, and he was sure death was creeping up on him in the form of exhaustion. But he wouldn't stop. Couldn't. Unlike most of his competitors, he didn't just dance because he wanted to. He had to. Dancing was everything to him. Had always been. But since he'd discovered that there was money attached to winning the competition, he danced because his education and future depended on it.

"Hey! I like the way you worked that routine. You was riding the heck outta that floor! Wonder who you was thinking about, bouncing up and down like that," a girl's voice sang from behind.

Ziggy shifted his feet in front of him, tied his shoes, then looked up. He already knew who was talking to him before he laid eyes on her. It was her. *Her. The* girl for him. The one with the always freshly twisted hair, banging body, and superior air about her. The one chick who'd moved into his brain last year and wouldn't go away.

"Thanks, but I could'a done better. I came up a lil' short on the spin," he said honestly as he stood.

"It looked good to me. Can you teach me?" She stood with her arms behind her back. Obviously clasping her hands, her chest poked a little in her pink leotard. Black formfitting tights rode her hips and cinched her tiny waist.

Ziggy looked at her. She was beautiful, bordering on skinny. But she had curves, serious ones, in all the right places. More importantly, he could pick her up and float her body through the air while they danced. Today, that was all he cared about. The competition and pricing the new dance shoes he needed, had been watching, but couldn't afford. Hopefully, they were on sale because he couldn't spring for them in addition to his monthly tuition if they weren't.

He reached for her, wondering who she was. Not her name. Not her art. He wanted to know *her*. What she liked. How he could keep her smiling like that. They'd never been formally introduced, and he didn't care. In a way, he didn't want to know what was on her birth certificate, her parents could've named her Skit Scat for all he cared. The truth was he liked his fantasy of her, and didn't want truth yet. Reality would make her one of his few, and she wasn't the few type. She was a keeper, he hoped.

What am I thinking? he questioned himself. This girl was making him too soft, way too cottony, and there was nothing pillow-like about him. He was Ziggy Phillip, the man, and he didn't do soft—unless it was a girl—but it'd be her, not him. He just enjoyed it.

"You're the choreographer here. So, how do you want me?" she asked, standing in front of him.

Ready. Willing. Able.

He waited for the track to change, then took her arms, pulled her to him. "Flow with me. Don't be afraid. It's only a dance, sweet girl." He took her hips in his palms, winded his midsection close to hers. They were only feather length apart. Not close enough to be nasty, not too far away to be acquainted. The hardwood was under their feet, feeling good to his soles. The smoothness of the floor and music had always proved to be the best cure for a bad day, was even better on one like today. An easy, fun one spent with someone who piqued his curiosity. Ziggy dragged the back of his hand along her neck, got into their groove. He could tell that, like him, dancing wasn't only her passion; it seemed to be her escape, just as it was his haven. It provided a chance for him to crawl into himself and think things through, plan his future as a choreographer, and figure out how to keep his parents from finding out he danced. His father knowing would equal career suicide.

"Just like that," he urged as she became his on the floor.

Her hips swayed rhythmically under his hold. Side to side, their midsections rocked while she grinded her rear into him, then let her upper body collapse forward. Catching her by her hair, pulling her close, Ziggy moved her head to one side, exposing her neck. His tongue, nearly touching her skin, traveled up to her jaw, and she seductively submitted. Gave in to the heat of the dance and him. He couldn't deny she was good. But together, they were better, he thought. Climbing his tight muscled body like a pole, she slid down him until their pelvises kissed, and he held her like a child with her legs wrapped around him. *Perfect synchronization?* The way she touched him, the way they grooved, was unbelievable. Their moves were so tight it was hard to tell where Ziggy ended and she began, he noticed as he watched them practice in the mirror. Another twirl. Third hip dip. A crawl, fetch and catch. And a dang-I-hate-to-unwrap-my-body-from-yours ended the routine.

Out of breath, Ziggy sank to the floor, wiped away his sweat, then closed his eyes. A small blast of cool air blew on his skin, and he opened his lids.

The girl sat next to him fanning with him a booklet. "You can work the heck outta that floor. Finally, you do know that, don't you?"

Ziggy smiled. "Yeah. I guess I do. Maybe always have. It's just that I can't afford to be too confident. I don't wanna lose it, ya know? It's all I got."

She moved her twists out of her face. "Oh, you got it

in a serious way, but don't ever believe it's all you got. That's how people fail—relying on one thing." She winked, and got up. "I'll see you next practice." And with that she walked away, picking up her backpack from the floor and making her way to the door.

"Hold up!" Ziggy yelled, then fell silent when he saw La-La come in the way the girl was going out. He'd changed his mind, wanted to know her name, but it was too late. In his life, La-La was on the rise, and he'd just asked her out the other day. He couldn't disrespect her or play himself. He told the girl never mind, then walked up to La-La. To his surprise, he was really as happy to see her as he had been to see the other the girl. His player card should've been snatched because twice in one week, he'd softened.

"Hey, pretty girl. What's good?" he asked, walking up to her.

La-La smiled. She was pretty, that was for sure. Too bad she didn't dance, he thought, sure she'd be easy to carry across the floor. "I didn't know you'd be in here. Rikki asked me to see if her bag's in here," she said, half apologetically.

He wrapped his arms around her, and she shrugged away.

"Z, you're sweating up a storm."

Ziggy smiled, then walked over by the door, and pulled a container of baby wipes from a shelf. "Yeah, yeah, I know. But a little sweat never killed anyone." He popped open the container, wiping perspiration from his body and face. "Let's go grab a snack and something to drink."

La-La crinkled her nose, laughing. "*Ill*. You do that, go out without bathing? That's nasty."

"No. What's nasty is walking around with a dry mouth and stank breath. Plus, it's a heat wave outside; everybody in New York is sweating. Probably funky too. Nobody will be able to tell."

They held hands and walked out the door, then collided with nosiness in its purest form, Nakeeda's super-huge-headed best friend. La-La looked at Ziggy, and he shook his head. "Hammerhead-Helen, what are you doing?"

Hammerhead-Helen sucked her teeth, and somehow managed to make her extremely large forehead stretch about two more inches. "Telling Nakeeda, that's what! I'm watching you, Ziggy," she said, walking away with a trail of toilet paper dangling out of her waistline.

8

JAMAICA-KINCAID

Jamaica pushed open the heavy steel door, and entered the school alone. Without Mateo by her side, she felt as if everyone was looking at her. She knew she was a spectacle, a stander-outer. There were only a few blondes with blue eyes there, but none resembled her. Well, rather, she didn't look like any of them. Her long honey locks flowed down her back, swiping against her James Perse T-shirt and worn Stella McCartney jeans. Her shoes weren't just any gym shoes, they were Lanvin sneakers. Everything about her screamed money, no matter how much she tried to downplay it. But the truth was, it didn't matter that her tee that looked like a regular Hanes cost fifty dollars, or that she rocked almost six-hundred-dollar jeans and seven-hundred-dollar sneakers, because she was still broke. Almost penniless, a month away from being homeless, and starving for something more than Ramen noodles, cheap cookies, and faucet water.

"Hey, Jamaica," someone greeted, walking past her in a flash.

Her stomach growled, reminding her that she hadn't eaten since yesterday and that, more than anything, she needed a job. Quick. She looked at her watch, then at the students who bustled through the hall. Class would begin in a few minutes, a room full of people that she wouldn't blend in with.

"S'up, Jamaica-Kincaid Ellison. Never would'a imagined a white girl pulling off locks, but you're rockin' yours. Rockin 'em," a black girl said, smiling. "Nice job on that scene the other day too. I might need to run lines with you."

Jamaica smiled, and said, "Thanks. Anytime. Anytime, just let me know when." Then she wished that other people saw her the way the girl had: as an artist, a girl with a nice do who was just a girl, not a white girl trying to blend into Harlem.

Continuing down the hall, Jamaica slipped into the cafeteria, and found her a seat in the corner of the room. She dropped her book bag on the table, whipped out her phone, and dialed her lifesaver. The line rang and rang, but no one answered. Where was her sister? She looked at her watch again. She definitely wasn't in class because, if Jamaica remembered her sister's schedule completely, her sister was in study hall. She shook her head. Her sister was in charge of the money—her money—and she needed some. Her stomach growled again, reminding her that she only had one dollar and forty-eight cents, a MetroCard credited with seven subway fares, a dream, and a *Backstage* magazine. Defeat etched her face. A lump grew in her throat. And a rising heat threatened to make her explode, fall all over her emotions, and cave in to self-pity. But she didn't have time to feel sorry for herself. She only had time to pull it together so she could get it together. She'd been scouring the actor's dream paper all morning, looking for every open audition only to be disappointed. There seemed to be no demand for new talent.

Disappointed, Jamaica picked up the paper and tossed it in the corner trash can. "Everybody wants agented actors." She stretched, her arms held high and her hopes low. She needed money to live and get her plan under way. There were only so many auditions she could make with seven train rides. With her sister ignoring her calls and not depositing money in her account, Jamaica didn't know how she would do it. Yes, she would get a job, she'd decided on that. But at her age she'd only qualify for a small-time gig that would equal an equivalently minute paycheck. That probably wouldn't be enough. She had to wrap her dainty fingers around hundreds to cover the rent, buy groceries, and make her rounds to get acting work. Definitely more mint-green paper than she had in her pocket.

"Don't tell me you're one of *them*." Mateo appeared next to her with crossed arms, waiting for an answer.

Jamaica looked at him, then began smiling but didn't know why. She could never figure out why he made her happy for no reason. "One of *who*?"

"Ya know, the *perfect* ones. Like the dancers—especially the ballerinas, the ones who sit in the cafeteria so they can *say* they went to lunch, but are so concerned about their weight that they don't eat. You missed the memo too? Perfection *doesn't* exist," he answered with a hint of a sparkle in his eye.

"You can't be serious, Mateo. *I* wrote the memo. I'm not acting like I'm going to lunch—I can't afford lunch! And I'm desperate."

Mateo ignored her words, picked up her bag from the seat, and walked away. "And I'm hungry and thirsty. Let's go get our eat on."

Jamaica was on his heels. "Wait! Where do you think your goin' with my bag?"

Mateo stopped. "Perfect *and* deaf too?" He laughed. "I told you already. We're goin' to get our munch on."

Out of breath, Jamaica was too tired to make excuses. "Listen, I can't go anywhere until I track down my sister," she explained. "Besides, you've done too much already. I need to pay my way."

Mateo turned back and winked. "So *pay* you shall. I'll make sure of it."

As they turned the corner, passersby still whizzed by them in blurs, their words just a jumble of nothing to her ears, just like Mateo's rants about some teacher. Jamaica slowed, tried to calm herself after she'd sent her sister a fifth text. She didn't want to appear frazzled when she got to wherever Mateo was taking her.

"*Here*," he said, stopping at a corner vending cart. Hotdogs, gyros, chicken on sticks topped off by bread. The food she'd once consider unsanitary now seemed delicious, and her stomach agreed, growling. "This is the *best* one in the city, *trust* me." He ordered for them both, then handed her the chicken on a stick that the vendor had sloshed with some sort of spicy barbecue sauce.

Jamaica almost swallowed the stick; she'd scarfed it down so fast, then licked her fingers. She couldn't help herself. In gulps, she dusted off the can of soda she and Mateo shared, then let out a loud belch. If her parents could only see her now, they'd lose everything holy about them.

"C'mon," Mateo urged, pulling her along. "We're almost there."

Almost where? she wanted to ask, but didn't. So far Mateo had made good on everything he'd ever said to her. She saw no need to question anything he said. She trusted him like a sibling—more than her sibling now that her sister was MIA with the money.

"*Here!*" he said, inflecting his word again. It was still a funny habit that she had to stop herself from laughing at. It was his quirk. Everyone was allowed at least one. "*This* is it."

Jamaica stood face-to-face with Starbucks, an old favorite from her Connecticut boarding school days. It now loomed in front of her like an enemy, taunting her about being broke and unable to afford the specialty coffees she'd once downed like free water. "Here? Not here . . ."

Mateo pulled her inside, then through the crowd of 'Buckies. It was as packed as all the others she'd been to, and the smell of coffee reminded her of how good she'd had it at her old boarding school.

"*Hey.*" Mateo waved to someone behind the counter,

then walked to the side of it and stood next to the employee door.

Jamaica noticed that some guy was waving back before Mateo snatched her by the arm, and pulled her with
him. Now they both stood in front of the door.

"Terrence! *My* man," Mateo said, giving him a pound
as soon as the door opened.

"What it do, bro?" Terrence asked, walking through
the door and leaning against the side counter.

Mateo nodded toward Jamaica. "This is *my* homegirl,
little sister, best *friend*. And she has something to ask
you." He turned to Jamaica. "Terrence is my boy, and
the *manager* here. Now *what* did you have to ask him
again . . . since you need to pay your way?"

Jamaica raised her brows, cringed a little, and swallowed her surprise. "Are you hiring?"

Terrence gave a sympathetic smile. "If you were over
sixteen, I could."

Her face fell, and she felt stupid. Hurt, even. "Okay."

"Stay right here while I'll bring you two some iced coffees. I was just getting ready to leave the plantation and
go meet my mom at the theater. There's some chick there
who's digging me hard," Terrence said.

Jamaica perked up. "Theater?"

Mateo smiled. "Forgot to tell you. *His* mom is *my*
mom's boss. She's in charge."

Jamaica nearly jumped across the counter when she
grabbed Terrence's hand. "I *am* old enough to be a stagehand. I'm sure of that. I can even work off the books.
Please!" she begged.

Terrence looked at Mateo. "You said she was determined." He turned to Jamaica. "Our boy here told me about you. We just had to see how much you wanted a job. If you were only willing to work in theater, I knew you weren't the type of employee my mom would tolerate. You have to be thirsty to work for her—and not a groupie. It's not going to be easy. Sometimes there's toilets, vomiting, fights—things a janitor or police aren't around for." He grinned, and nodded. Did everything but give her a verbal yes. But his walking out the door and motioning for them to follow him was all the affirmation she needed. She was going to get her a job even if she had to get on bended knee and beg. Acting like a beggar would be easy.

Jamaica wrapped her arms around Mateo, then got on tiptoe and kissed him on the cheek. "Thanks. I owe you big time."

"And you'll pay . . . big time," he said, laughing.

9

LA-LA

La-La hoisted her book bag over her shoulder as she crossed the street as quickly and safely as she could. She was running behind. She looked at her watch. Remi's chemo treatment was almost over, and she'd promised her that morning she'd make it in time to keep her company while she was connected to the infuser. Zigzagging through the pedestrians, she exhaled the breath she'd been holding. She was only two buildings away from the hospital. "Better late than never," she said to make herself feel better about her tardiness, but it didn't work. She should've been there, she chastised, but there was nothing she could do. She couldn't cut class, especially not Mrs. Allen's. Mrs. Allen didn't play—ever—and La-La'd bet the grouchy lady hadn't even done so as a child. In fact, she couldn't imagine her ever being young. "A dollar to a dime, she was born old and grumpy," La-La began, but was cut off by something heavy whizzing over her shoulder that made her stop dead in her tracks. "What the—?" Something else whooshed by her, harder this time. *A rock?*

"So you think you can *sang*, hunh?" Nakeeda's voice came from behind, joined by giggles.

La-La cringed. Today was not the day and now was not the time. She turned and her eyes widened. Nakeeda stood less than a half block away with at least six other girls flanking her sides, and Hammerhead-Helen, with her huge forehead and nappy edges, stood out from the rest. Even from where La-La stood, she could feel the weight of Hammerhead's dome. All the girls were holding what appeared to be rocks and bricks. Her heart moved into her throat and beat until she could feel it in her temples. Then it raced, making her blood pulse. Her hands sweated as she gripped the strap of the book bag. She shook her head. She hated being scared, and wished she could find the courage—the strength—to knock some sense into Nakeeda and Hammerhead-Helen. But even if she could, she wouldn't. She was no fool, and knew she couldn't handle seven girls.

"Oh, I don't see you talking junk now! No Cyd to back you up this time." Nakeeda aimed another rock, then threw it like a missile.

La-La jumped to the side, dodging it. "Stop, Nakeeda! I gotta go pick up my sister."

The girls fell out in laughter, Nakeeda the lead and the loudest. "Oh, your poor little sister. What's wrong with baldilocks now? I heard your momma over-processed her hair trying to make her look like your step-daddy's child!"

The gang of girls roared in laughter now.

La-La roared too, but it wasn't laughter coursing through her. It was anger. Nobody bothered Remi. *Nobody*. They'd somehow managed to keep Remi's illness a secret or, at least, she thought they did. La-La took Nakeeda's tease to heart.

"Shut up, Nakeeda!" she spewed her anger for the first time, then caught herself. She didn't have time to play into Nakeeda's stupidity; she had to get to Remi. Hoisting her bag over her shoulder again, she turned her back to Nakeeda and her crew, and walked toward the hospital. A couple more large rocks flew past her, but she kept going. She had to. Remi's problem was bigger than Nakeeda.

The cab pulled up to their project building, and Remi sprung from it as if she hadn't just had one poison funneled into her veins to kill another. La-La watched her in awe, and was mad at their mother for not making the appointment. Again. But, as usual, Boom-Kesha was pregnant, and now couldn't be around "sick" people as she'd so unkindly put it.

"You sure you don't want me to walk you in, Remi? I have time, you know. Cyd's house isn't going anywhere," La-La offered, still sitting in the cab.

Remi tightened the knot on her headscarf, the edges of her hair gone as if they'd never been there. "I'm good. I won't feel bad or weak for a while. *But*, if you must do something for me," she said, patting the scarf, "you can trade me your hair," she teased. "That'd be hot, La-La.

We could be twins! Tell Cyd I said what-it-is, and go let her hook you up with a look for your upcoming date," she said, laughing.

La-La asked the cabbie to wait, then stepped out. Quickly, she gave Remi a hug, then hustled back before the driver lost his patience. "Deal! Deal! And Deal!" she yelled out, then smiled as the taxi pulled off. She could still hear her sister's laughter.

She was ready for her date. Well, mentally ready, but not physically. "Okay," she said, holding up her hands. "I'm your guinea pig. Work your magic." She looked around. Clothes were strewn all over the place. CDs were in semi-neat stacks on the dresser. Shoes were lined up against the wall according to color and style. La-La took in the posters on the wall, topped by various hats hung over them, and admired every sexy singer and rapper imaginable. Every time she entered Cyd's room, she saw something new. "Cyd, you have your own mini mall in here," she said, plopping down in a fuzzy orange chair, then realizing Cyd was still digging around in the closet.

"Got it!" Cyd said, emerging from the closet with blue, red, yellow, and green fabrics draped over her arm.

La-La's eyes bulged. She was here to get help, not do worse than she could on her own. "Cyd, you don't mean that, right? I'm not going out with Ziggy looking like birthday-party balloons. What's up with all the colors?"

Cyd cradled the clothes in one arm, and put her free hand on her hip. She cocked her head to the side, then sucked her teeth. "Talk about ungrateful? Dag! The red is for you. It'll make you pop." She held a finger to her lip in thought, walking over to La-La. She fingered her hair. "Especially if we tease this into a real retro, funky style."

La-La's eyebrows shot up. Cyd was going to kill her.

Cyd gave her the side-eye. "*What?*"

"Can't I just wear one of your hats, or can you wrap it, you know . . . in one of those African-like head wraps?"

Cyd walked over and dumped the armload of clothes onto the bed. She pivoted as if she were modeling, then closed her eyes and took a deep breath. She held it, obviously trying to hold in her frustration. "What. Is. The. Problem. La-La?" she sputtered, exhaling.

"Well, I was thinking . . . I think I want to cut my hair."

Cyd pushed La-La's head back. "Shuddup! You're not cutting your hair. Besides, your boy Ziggy seems to love it."

La-La pressed her lips together as she weighed the decision. Yes, Ziggy did love her hair, was always complimenting her on it, and it was all she physically had to get his attention. "Maybe later?"

"Maybe you can just let me work my magic, and get you right. After I'm done with you, Ziggy'll forget he ever wanted anyone else."

10

REESE

Unnoticed, Reese slipped out of the apartment as easily as she'd walked in minutes before. She knew she was pushing it, but was at ease knowing her mother was dead to the world, almost comatose thanks to a long day at work and a training session at the gym, and seven-year-old Dakota was snoring and babbling his dreams aloud, so Reese didn't have to babysit him, she reasoned. But even if her mom and nephew were up, Reese wouldn't have cared. Not after Blaze had called, romanced her with an apology, promised to stop his stupid activity and work on hot tracks with her. He'd begged her to come out to play, and lured her with a hypnotic beat over the line. The thick bass and his smooth tone had erased every second of anger she'd ever felt, every single instance of her questioning staying with him. His admission of guilt for standing her up was so sweet it'd made her shrug out of her comfy pj's and into a summer getup, grab her purse, and make a quiet exit. She wanted to look good for him, especially after he'd upped the lure with a dangle of a hot surprise. The bad-boy swagger that she was so attracted to pulled her into the Harlem night, where she waited for him by the train station around the corner from her co-op.

Leaned against a building, Reese wrapped her arms around her body to kill the late-night chill. A skinny, micro-mini low-rider skirt and slices of fabric crisscrossing her breasts were no match for the cool wind. But she smiled anyway.

A glance at her watch told her he was five minutes late, and she began to worry. He'd stood her up twice, and hadn't really apologized until tonight.

A black Mercedes with midnight-tinted windows screeched to a stop and idled in front of where she stood. Then the engine roared. Purred. Growled. Then finally hummed again. No one exited the car. Reese studied her surroundings, and fear crept in. She was in the city that was never supposed to sleep, yet there wasn't a soul around. It was just her and that car. And the eerie click-click sound it was now making. Someone on the inside of it was playing with the locks.

Reese about-faced, fighting against the wind as her footfalls quickly carried her toward the corner. She may have been born into an overprotective household, but she was no fool. She knew if caught alone at night by the wrong person, the city streets would eat her alive.

In seconds, the Mercedes drove up beside her. And Reese panicked. Started kicking up dust as she ran as fast as she could.

"Hey!" a male voice yelled out to her from the open car window as it kept pace with her.

But the wind whirred in her ears, and Reese couldn't tell to whom the voice belonged.

"Yo! Where ya running to? Told you I had a surprise!" The car pulled over and parked.

Reese stopped and stared at a smiling Blaze. "Who let you drive their car, B?" she asked, shedding her fear, and sauntering toward the driver's side.

"*I* let me. This is my whip. Like it?"

Reese smiled, forgetting he'd just scared the wits out of her, and ignoring how she knew he'd paid for the car. "Yeah. It's hot. Can I drive it?" She bit her bottom lip.

"You can ride—I mean, ride in it."

She was under a bridge by the Harlem River before she knew it. Her back was pressed against the car door as Blaze stood in front of her. "So you're serious about the music and everything?" asked Reese.

"Yep." Without pause, Blaze reached into his pocket, retrieved a cigar. With the precision of a razor blade, his thumbnail sank into the brown paper, slicing it open. Dumping the tobacco on the ground, he removed the lining, filled it with his junk. Rolled it, licked it, twisted the ends. Blazed up. Winked. Blew smoke in Reese's face.

"Are you freakin' crazy or something, B? You just told me you'd stop." She pushed him away, then got back into the car.

He mumbled under his breath, then followed suit. He walked around the car, and got in on the driver's side. In seconds, the engine purred, and the car pulled off. Blaze continued to smoke like he was alone; then he did it again. While turning the corner, he blew smoke in Reese's face.

Reese did something she knew was stupid. She grabbed the gear shift, threw the car in park even though it was still moving.

There was a screech and grind. Blaze jerked forward, his chest connecting with the steering wheel. The green he held hit the windshield and bits of fire rained down, turning to ash before they hit the dash. "What the f—?" He threw the car back into driving gear, saving his precious transmission on his dirty-money-purchased Mercedes. "You lost your f'n mind or something?" he yelled.

Reese shook her head. She'd never heard of a drug dealer who refused to curse. Blaze was fake. Window dressing that looked good from the outside, perpetrating to be the real thing. "Have *I* lost my mind? Right. You're the one who says one thing then does another . . . and believes both—which is crazy, remember? That ain't cool, B. And neither is this dirty-money car. It's a ride that's gonna depreciate and hit bottom. If you want to invest, invest in you—our music, and education. Or are you too high to remember how?"

Blaze whipped the car to the curb and threw it in park. "Get out!"

"*What?*" Reese knew she'd heard wrong. No way he going to put her out on the street like a stray dog. He must've forgotten who she was and the small fact that she was supposed to be important to him.

He picked up his clip and blazed up again. Choking, he caught his breath and said: "Look Reese. You're too good for me—you want things I just don't find too impor-

tant. Yes, I'm smart, but I'm not interested in college . . .
or music like that, nothing's ever coming from it. Your
passion is a hobby, Reese."

Reese went slightly deaf after the not-interested statement. She didn't need to hear more. She sat erect, and
held up her hand in a stop sign. "You know what, you're
right. Let me out. Here."

He cursed. It was a small one, but still one. "No. I'm
going to take you back where I—"

"Here! Let me out here," she demanded, throwing the
moving car in park again.

"Okay, just let me get you to a well-lit area. That's all I
ask. I may not always think right, but give me some
credit," he said, and she listened because the street was
too dark.

The few blocks seemed like a small eternity, though
they were only a mile or two from a suitable place. Distance crawled by, people seemed to be tipping on their
toes, and the few trees planted in the middle of the walk
didn't bend in the wind. Everything moved slowly because she wanted to be out of the car and away from
Blaze. He'd sounded one-track-minded just like her father, only thinking about work and money. He didn't
take her talent seriously, yet she'd done everything to
prove that she was serious. Well, almost everything. She
snuck out every chance she could to practice because
other than playing around on GarageBand on her laptop,
that was the only way she could get some serious work
in. She'd studied the greatest producers such as TR from
Ultramagnetic MCs, Primo, and The Roots, some who
sampled and the others who didn't. She'd done every-

thing she could except brand the words *I Produce* on her forehead, and she was seriously considering doing just that just to put her dad's shorts in a twist and show her mom that she wasn't the reincarnation of her mom's childhood. And Blaze had the nerve to call her music a hobby? Heck, *he* was the hobby—a phase, fad, so last year.

"Credit given," she said, stepping from the car and onto the curb. Her phone vibrated before she could slam the passenger door. A text was coming through. She pressed the button under the READ highlighted on the cell screen; then her mouth went dry.

Where r u? Dakota woke up your mom!!! A text from Wheezy.

"Hey . . . Reese, right?" the Jamaican boy from the vending table on One-two-five asked. The same guy with the hard bass beats that she needed and could no longer get from Blaze.

Reese looked at the text, then back to the guy. *What to do? What to do?* she mentally asked herself. She was already going to be on punishment; should she make it worth it? A couple of hours more wouldn't hurt.

11

ZIGGY

Cars blurred by, spitting puddle water on the sidewalk. Ziggy cursed under his breath, grabbed the few leather bootleg designer bags that were on the front of the vending table, and inspected them for damage. Sure enough, the spray of dirty drops had hit the bags, ruining one red one and two natural-colored ones. His mind clicked, calculating numbers, and he could already feel the fifty-dollar loss he'd have to take for the damage. If he were lucky, he'd be able to discount them, but there was no way he could sell them at full price. Not now, unless some unsuspecting tourist snatched them up, which was all he could hope for. He was already short on his tuition money.

Snapping his fingers, he signaled Broke-Up.

No answer.

Again he snapped his fingers, popping them as loud as possible, but the music was too loud, and it was raising his irritation. He didn't know how his brother could think or be productive with all that noise. How on earth did he talk to the customers if he couldn't hear? "Broke-Up! Broke-Up!"

"What you yelling for, Z?" Broke-Up finally turned the music down and asked.

Holding one of the tan purses as if it were a baby, Ziggy looked at his brother like he had an ear in the middle of his forehead. "Pass me the leather cleaner and a rag, yo."

Broke-Up put his fingertips down on the table with his fingers spread. He returned Ziggy's crazy look. "'Yo' nothing. What ya deal with, Ziggy? Why are you looking at me like that?"

A face-off between the brothers was brewing, and Ziggy could feel it in his bones. Sometimes Broke-Up just rode his nerve, but he couldn't say anything because he wasn't doing Broke-Up a favor, it was the other way around. Still though, his brother's ways bothered him. Like now, after he'd asked for leather cleaner, Broke-Up was too concerned with turning up the music.

"I feel your eyes on my back, Z. Don't mess up my day. I met this pretty Coolie-looking chick with long hair, some producer gal, and I ran into her again last night. I'm sure I can bag her, been thinking about how to make my move when I see her again, and you're ruining my vibe with your attitude."

Now Ziggy had to laugh. Broke-Up met a lot of people, but he never bagged girls. Pulling cuties just wasn't one of his strengths. Sure, he tried, but usually his knees got in the way. Literally. Almost doubling over in laughter, Ziggy said, "Yo, Broke-Up, remember when you tripped trying to catch up to that girl? You needed to have your pins oiled or something."

Broke-Up banged his fist on the vending table, making the purses and CDs jump. "Don't play me, Z. I can pull this girl, I know I can. She likes my music. She's some girl who goes to that Harlem performing arts school or whatever the name of it is. Reese. That's her name."

Ziggy swallowed his laughter, and coughed. *Did he just say Reese?* Worry filled him until it overflowed. He cleared his throat, hocked up phlegm, then spat. He'd caught his breath, but that was all. *How in the . . . ?* "Broke-Up, stay away from them artsy girls, they're flakes. You want a girl you can count on. Let me find you—"

"No, Z. I want *her*. I think we can really vibe. Ya know?" Broke-Up said, digging in his pocket. He pulled out a wad of ones, fives, and tens. "Here's what we did earlier."

Ziggy took and counted the money. There still wasn't enough to pay his tuition yet, but he didn't panic. He still had a week or so. Folding the bills, he stuck them in his pocket alongside the fear of Broke-Up finding out about him through Reese. "Cool. Thanks. I'm going to take this to Canal Street and get some more bootleg bags. We gotta make more dough, Broke-Up. We gotta take advantage of this table."

Broke-Up gestured for him to hold up. "Another thing, Z. The cops been around here checking vending licenses lately. You gonna have to get a new one from Sandman.

You can tell ours is fake. We should've spent with Sandman, and we wouldn't be having these problems."

The bottle was housed in a paper bag with the top if it crinkled and bunched around the mouth. Ziggy gripped it tightly, and took a swig of it. He knew he was taking his chances as the beat cops walked down the street toward him. They'd think it was a beer, but he didn't care. He was in no mood to please or cater to anyone. He'd been doing that for years, hiding his art to make his parents—no, to make his father—happy, and he was tired. So what if he danced? Did that really make him the sissy his dad liked to call guys in dance shoes? And what was up with the whole straight-dudes-don't-dance thing, anyway? What was the deal with the men in his family being so homophobic? They were a hate group that taught Ziggy and all his male relatives to hate what they hated, but the truth was Ziggy didn't dislike anyone, and saw no reason to judge. He didn't care if all the guys who wore ballet shoes alongside him liked girls or boys, all that mattered to him was if they could dance or not. Talent was important to him, not preference.

"What's the 911, Z?" Rikki asked, walking up to him.

"What's in the bag, son?" a cop asked, reaching him seconds after Rikki.

Ziggy looked at Rikki, and she shook her head in the negative, begging him with her eyes not to get smart. He sucked his teeth, then swigged his soda from the bottle. His eyes were on the police officer the whole time.

"You hear me?" The cop walked up on him, snatched

him by the collar, then pressed him against the building. "What's in the bag? A Heineken?" He snatched Ziggy's drink. "You're a little young to be drinking. What else you got on you?" he quizzed, pulling the bottle out of the bag.

Ziggy watched him, wide-eyed and daring. He wasn't scared of the police. Had never feared the streets or authority. Nothing put fear in his heart, except his dad finding out he danced.

"You little . . ." The cop stopped himself from cursing, then handed Ziggy back his soda. "I should take you in just for being so smart."

Ziggy snatched the drink. "You can't. You know it and I know it."

"Sorry, officer," Rikki said, pulling Ziggy away. As soon as she had him around the corner, she pushed him into a parked car. "What's wrong with you, Z? Are you trying to go to jail or get the mess beat out of you?"

He looked at her, blinking hard. He was so mad tears wanted to come, but he couldn't cry. Men in his family weren't allowed to do that either. "Broke-Up met Reese, and now he wants to holler at her. Something about her being a producer too. You know about that?"

Rikki reared back her head in disbelief. "You mean our Reese? Like Harlem CAPA's classical pianist and almost-every-other-instrument-playing Reese?"

His look answered yes.

"Well, we gotta stop that before it gets started, Z. You got the competition coming up, and if your dad finds out . . ."

"If my dad finds out there won't be a competition for me—maybe not a family or home either. And if I can't get my hands on a more authentic-looking vending license, it won't matter anyway because I won't be able to afford CAPA."

12

JAMAICA-KINCAID

They strode through the hall arm in arm, more like boyfriend and girlfriend instead of BFFs. With all the attention they were getting, Jamaica was sure everyone else thought so too. She looked over at Mateo, smiled, and shook her head. He was eating it up.

"So, what are you doing *later*?"

Jamaica gave him the side eye.

"Oops, *working*! I forgot."

Acting class was next, so Jamaica was in a good mood, and decided not to punch him in the arm like she usually would. "This way. . . . Your groupie's waiting."

Mateo pulled away. "Not today. I don't want to lay eyes on *Hammerhead*-Helen today or *ever*, and I don't feel like acting *or* dealing with Mr. Sassafras."

Jamaica burst out laughing. "Mr. Sassafric," she corrected. Their acting teacher was over the top in every way imaginable. She thought it was hilarious, and enjoyed him. Mateo was just the polar opposite. He could live without Mr. Sassafric and all his antics. He hated the way the teacher spoke, dressed, and sipped his tea with his pinky finger raised. He had a bad word for everything Mr. S. did, but act. Now that even Mateo couldn't deny. Mr. S's acting and his ability to develop his students were ridiculous in a great way.

Jamaica pushed open the door, made an entrance with Mateo still on her arm. Without thought, she dropped her bag on a seat, and Mateo walked her up the few steps to the stage, where she took her place. She longed for the lights, craved instruction, and wanted to cry daily just because she had the acting skills to do so. And Mr. Sassafric catered to her every need. She looked to her right, smiled at the guy she was going to run the scene with, then to her left and laid eyes on Hammerhead-Helen, who felt just the opposite of their teacher.

Making a production of it, Mateo kissed her on the cheek and whispered in her ear. "She *hates* you. You know that, don't you?" he said, laughing and walking away.

Two hand claps signaled the beginning of class. Mr. S. stood in front of the stage with his thin lips pressed together. Jamaica looked at his getup of the day. Burnt-orange pants, old-school white espadrille shoes with straw bottoms, and a flowery button-down with a tight checkered T-shirt underneath, almost choking his neck, and the checkers matching neither his clothes nor his shoes. His hair was moussed to a crisp wisp in the middle of his head, making him resemble an old Alfalfa from *The Little Rascals*. She loved his style. He didn't care what anyone thought, and she thought that was admirable. Fingering her own locks, she could dig his uniqueness.

"Tea, please."

Jamaica shot Mateo a look, saw he was feigning vomiting, and she fell out laughing, breaking her character before she got into it.

"Jamaica-Kincaid," Mr. S. tsked, shaking his head slowly. "Cry for me. In five, four, three, two . . ." He snapped his fingers.

And the tears burst like a dam. Without work, without hesitation, Jamaica's eyes reddened, her nose ran, her cheeks flushed. Her breath even caught, making her gasp for air like she'd hurt herself something awful. She cried, then smiled, turning it off like she'd hadn't just seemed like the saddest person alive.

"Laugh like you've just heard the funniest thing in the world. In five, four, three, two . . ."

Laugh, she did. She cracked up until the tears came again.

"Be sad . . ."

"Now anger . . ."

"Now somberness . . ."

"Happiness, Jamaica. Give us happy. Now give us death. . . ."

She and Mr. S. went in and out of emotion as if they were the only two in the room. For every emotion he requested, she delivered.

"Now sing. Sing like you're a Grammy Award–winning star. We're your audience, the people you owe your fame to."

With a voice worse than she believed anyone should be cursed with, Jamaica opened her mouth and belted out Billie Holiday's "Ain't Nobody's Business If I Do." Back and forth across the stage, she strutted, taking hands and shaking them as if the students were really her fans, and some of them were. Most were, except Hammerhead-Helen. Jamaica decided to have fun, hoping that Mr. S. would do what she predicted he would. She strutted over to her enemy, singing and grabbing her hand, and stayed in front of her belting what she knew was the most awful rendition of Billie Holiday.

"Helen, act! Swoon. Pass out. Jamaica is your favorite star—pay her homage."

With mouth still wide, Jamaica managed to smile, and almost broke character when Hammerhead-Helen had to fall to her knees. Then she walked away, leaving her hater in her trail.

Mateo stood, clapping the loudest and the longest, tears streaming from his eyes. "*My* baby is a *star* . . . right, *Hammer* . . . Helen?" he asked, catching his slip before he could finish.

Mr. S. turned and looked at Mateo. He nodded. "Yes. Yes, she is."

Jamaica ran as fast as she could. Her job was only two blocks away, and she had to beat feet to get there. She was running late, but would make it in time. She took everything she did seriously. She wasn't sure if it was because of her parents and how they'd raised her or because of the boarding school and how they'd demanded she conduct herself. Whatever reason, it was ingrained in her.

"Sorry," she yelled to the man she'd just collided with, sure she'd knocked his phone from his hand. Turning the corner, Jamaica lengthened her strides, turned left into the alley, and bounded toward the backstage entrance. She pounded on the door with all her might until she heard steps on the other side.

"Well, come in. Why are you so flushed and sweaty?" the head stagehand asked. Her name was Madeline, and she looked like a Madeline. Everything about her screamed prep and kisser-upper. She had a clipboard under her arm, surely the assignments for the day.

"Didn't want to be late," Jamaica explained.

Madeline shrugged, then looked at her watch. "Well, technically, Ms. Ellison, you're not late. However, you're late for the good assignments. I passed those out minutes ago. You have bathroom, dressing room, serving, and clean-up duty. Pretty much everything that's not really stagehand work."

13

LA-LA

She wrung her hands together, trying to twist the nervous sweat from her palms. If only she could wring them out like a sponge, her day would move faster. Her heart palpitated, beating off rhythm, and she was sure her date was over before it started due to her being the youngest stroke victim ever.

"What's up, La-La?" Ziggy greeted, walking up to her.

La-La's heart raced and butterflies flew in her chest, and she knew she wasn't going to have a stroke. She was just fine. And so was Ziggy, she noticed, watching how soft his lips looked today. "Hey!" She slammed shut her locker, held her books up to her flat chest to cover it. Hopefully, if he didn't see it, he'd forget that she didn't have any ta-tas to speak of.

Ziggy cocked his head to the side. "You stealing my manhood already?" he asked, taking the books from her.

"What kind of man would I be if I didn't carry your books?"

She swallowed so hard she was sure he could hear it. Then she somehow lifted her eyes to look at him. He was fine. "Man . . . ?" *Yes, a F. I. N. E. man. Maybe my man.*

"Of course, I'm a man. If I wasn't, you wouldn't let me take you out this weekend. Or kiss you."

Kiss? Did he say kiss? Any self-confidence she had died with only four letters. She began to panic, then tried to calm herself. She couldn't spaz in front of Ziggy. She just couldn't. But how could she stop herself knowing she hadn't ever lip-locked before?

"Oh, you with her?" Nakeeda's irritating voice sliced La-La's thoughts. "Hunh, Ziggy?"

Ziggy looked from Nakeeda to La-La. He shook his head. "Why? You been with everyone else. I mean *every-body.* So why can't I be with whoever I want?"

La-La stopped and took it all in. So Ziggy and Na-keeda had had something? She couldn't be sure, but it definitely seemed like it.

Nakeeda walked up to them, popping gum and smiling wickedly as if the devil were pulling up the corners of her lips. She put her hand on her hip, and looked La-La up and down. She cut her eyes at Ziggy, running her hand up and down her side, emphasizing her curves. "You know she can't give you what I can. How are you going to pass up all of this for *that*?"

La-La just shook her head. She wasn't going to play in to Nakeeda's shenanigans.

"Go somewhere, Nakeeda," Ziggy said, taking La-La by the hand and walking around Nakeeda.

"Maybe I'll *go* to the hospital to check on baldilocks." Nakeeda snickered.

La-La's head almost snapped off, she turned it so fast.

"What?" Ziggy asked. "Who?"

La-La pulled away from his hold, then walked over to Nakeeda. For the first time in her life, she was face-to-face with trouble, and she wasn't scared. "Let me tell you something, Luci. The next time you mention my sister—"

Ziggy pulled La-La away. "That's what she wants."

Nakeeda laughed. "Luci? Who's Luci? You so shook, you don't know what you're saying."

La-La looked over her shoulder, and stared Nakeeda in her eyes. She didn't blink. "Oh, I know what I'm saying. *You're* Luci—short for Lucifer, the devil. And for your information, I have plenty to give Ziggy. Maybe not your physical curves, but"—she pointed to her head—"these curves. My cerebral ones. You know, like cerebellum? It's called a brain." She huffed, scared out of her wits, but not of Nakeeda. She was afraid of the upcoming kiss. She needed to find Cyd and Rikki, they had a lot to accomplish in fifth period.

"Okay, here's how you do it. Pay close attention," Rikki instructed from where she sat on the floor of an empty classroom, holding half of a pitted peach.

La-La watched her closely. Rikki tilted her head, and closed her eyes as she pressed her parted lips against the fruit's circular opening, then kissed it.

"You see, La-La?" She sighed with a playful smirk, pulling the peach from her mouth. "It's easy. Just pucker, open slightly, and voila. The key to it is your lips. You've gotta open your mouth just right."

"We couldn't see how you moved your tongue," said Cyd. Her head was tilted, looking like she was anticipating more.

La-La shook her head. "I couldn't see your tongue. How do you know how to move your tongue?"

"Girl, please! Don't worry about that. It's just a dance. Follow Ziggy's lead, and you'll be fine. Trust me, that's how I learned—not from Ziggy, though. My boyfriend taught me, and he didn't even know it. I just did what he did." She batted her almond-shaped eyes that were enhanced by her stunning caramel complexion and long curls. "A dance?"

"Yes, silly. Tongue dancing. There's a rhythm to it, you know, just like doing *it* . . . well, just like dancing." She giggled infectiously.

La-La joined Rikki in her laughter. Then Cyd followed, crossing her eyes at La-La. Neither of them knew anything about the rhythm of *it*—meaning sex—but they'd read about it in *Cosmo* and other women's magazines. While Cyd had kissed before, and swore she'd almost mastered it, she admitted that she didn't know how to do it correctly—with her mouth open—the way that Rikki did.

"La-La's never kissed anybody—not even with her mouth closed," Cyd snitched.

Rikki cleared her throat. "First time for everything," she said, handing the other half of the fruit to La-La. "Go ahead."

La-La squirmed. It was her turn to tongue dance with

her half of the peach. She tried to mimic Rikki's demon-stration, but got too much into character. She'd mistaken the peach's mouth for Ziggy's, became more artsy and passionate with her performance, and squeezed the fruit too hard. The juices outlined her lips and dribbled down her chin. She couldn't help it; it was as succulent as she was sure Ziggy's mouth was.

All three doubled over in laughter.

"You're going to require more work than I thought," Rikki teased.

La-La wiped juice from her chin. "I'll never get it right."

"Well, you better, because here comes your dance part-ner," she said, nodding toward the door where Ziggy was peering inside the small rectangular window in the door.

"Hey, La-La, you wanna go to a pool party this week-end at my cousin's in Brooklyn? It's a cookout too."

She smiled and nodded.

After he left she said, "Oh gawd. Now what am I going to do? I can't go to a pool party with a case of the flats. I got a flat chest, flat butt, and I flat-out don't know how to kiss yet."

Rikki winked, then waved away La-La's concern. "Just go out, concentrate on letting him show you how to kiss, and, as far as the pool party—I got'chu. But you won't be wearing a bathing suit. I know what'll accentuate your positives."

14

REESE

Serious? Reese grimaced. One too many thought-piercing crunches interrupting her thinking. She looked sideways at Wheez, watched as she devoured a third apple in a row. Her teeth tore through the fruit as if it was the last meal she'd have, and she was enjoying it like Thanksgiving. Reese looked over to her snack of choice, a tray of delicious cupcakes she couldn't get enough of.

Crunch.

Wheez tore into the apple again, sending juice flying through the air, landing on Reese's face. Reese wiped away juice with the back of her arm. "Wheez, please! Enough with the apple already, Eve! *Jeez.* It's like the Garden of Eden around here with all these apples." She laughed, grabbed a cupcake, then Wheez's miniature binoculars they used to watch fights and other interesting happenings that took place on One hundred twenty-fifth Street below. She walked over to Wheez's bedroom win-

dow, and moved back the curtains for the umpteenth
time.

"How'd you skate around punishment again? I'm still
not sure how you got over here. I was sure you'd be
grounded forever."

"My mom knocked back out before I got in, and I convinced her she'd dreamed it all," Reese explained, binoculars on her face like an extension of her eyes. She
shivered. How close she'd come to what she was sure
would have been permanent lockdown still made her uncomfortable, but then she remembered something else
from that night: hanging out with Broke-Up. A smile
spread. She did let him see her home, though she'd been
too scared to give him her number or take his. She hadn't
even hinted at them working together, or digging deeper
to find out if he really produced too. She shrugged.

"What's out there that's so interesting, all of a sudden?
Sandman out there on his soapbox preaching, singing,
and selling stuff again?" Wheez asked, sitting on the edge
of the bed.

Reese shook her head. She couldn't tell anyone what
had her attention—better yet, *who* had her attention.
Nope, not even Wheez, and they shared everything. She
would never admit to something she could hardly believe
herself. She had a secret. A deep, delicious never-tell-a-
soul secret that'd kept her fingers glued to the miniature
binoculars she had pressed against her face. Inhaling a
second chocolate-buttercream cupcake, she zoomed in
on her target. Greedily watched and consumed pleasure
with her eyes. Licking frosting from her lips, she tried to
back away from the window. Wanted to chuck the binoc-

ulars onto Wheez's unmade bed so they could get ready
for Julliard's classical concert being held in Central Park.
But she couldn't move. Wasn't able to free her hand of
the prized magnifiers. She needed one more look. Had to
have another moment to mentally savor the flavor of the
school year she'd craved since running into him again.
The forbidden taste of *ooh-la-la* she could only imagine.
And she couldn't stop her stomach from fluttering whenever she saw or thought about him. *Butterflies.*

"Drop two tears in a bucket and mutha'funk it," Reese
accidentally muttered her and Wheez's favorite cry-and-
get-over-it truism. Pulling herself from the window, she
collapsed onto the unmade bed, letting the binoculars fall
wherever. Instinctively, her fingers moved to her hair,
fanned out, raked across her scalp in aggravation. Who
was she to think she'd ever be good enough to work with
him? Bold enough to make a move on the guy she couldn't
stop watching from Wheez's window?

"I'm Reese. I *am* a hot producer, and the best thing
walking," she whispered the mantra Wheez had sug-
gested, then reached over and picked up the gift Wheez
had given her for a past birthday. A well-worn book Rus-
sell Simmons had written on accomplishment. The book
that told her her faith in herself, good deeds, and talent
was enough to get her to her destination.

"So you think you just gonna lay there and not tell?"
Wheez hovered over her with raised eyebrows. "Well,
I'm waiting." She crossed her arms, still holding an apple.

Rolling over onto her side, Reese grabbed a third cupcake from the nightstand, and sank her teeth into it. Enjoyed the sumptuous sweetness of the smooth chocolate

as it soothed her irritation. She didn't want to attend the concert or meet the orchestra maestro. *Ever*. Had no desire to be her mom's puppet she could dress up and push to the music elite like some new must-have prescription drug. No, Reese didn't want to be phony and superficial, but she couldn't help herself. Not only did she have no choice in the matter, her mother had baited her with an offer too sweet not to bite. If Reese accompanied Mrs. Allen to the concert she'd promised to buy Reese new software for her music. Mrs. Allen just had no idea that she would be buying Pro Tools, a must-have for any serious producer. She slid the book under the pillow, and her eyes zoomed in on the sleeveless blood-red outfit hanging on the closet door, then lit. She'd loved the getup from first sight, and had used it against her mother as a dangler. *If you pay for the software* and *buy me that outfit . . .*

Wheez was in her face now. "So . . . ?"

Reese just blinked, and shrugged her shoulders. "Fair exchange." *No robbery*. She shook away any negativity she had, and rolled off the bed, still ignoring Wheez, who was almost hyperventilating from nosiness. The concert, no matter how dull, would be great. For her. She convinced herself. Grabbing the outfit, she held it in front of her, practiced the perfect smile she'd worked on all week. She posed.

"Look Wheez, I'm saucy!" she exclaimed, praising herself. Carefully, she laid the stunning outfit across the bed and admired it again. She imagined what it'd look like tonight under the lights her mother would no doubt find a way to drag her under.

"La La Land," Wheez muttered, biting her apple.

"Wake up, Reese. Wake up and tell me what's up. Or else"—she snatched the outfit from the bed, ran the few feet to the window, and pushed the outfit through it—"this is going to fly five stories."

Reese rolled her eyes, then puckered her lips and blew air kisses to no one. "Okay, okay already. But if you tell a soul, I'm going to kill you, bring you back to life, then kill you again." She stuck out her hand. "Give first, then I'll give."

Wheez took the barter, and handed Reese the outfit. She plopped back onto the unmade bed, and crossed her arms and legs at the same time.

"There's this dude—"

Wheez jumped up like she was on fire, fanning herself. Reese rolled and crossed her eyes, waiting for Wheez to catch ablaze in any second. That, or start whirring like a siren. "Who? 'Cause 'this dude' definitely doesn't sound like B, Blaze, or any other nickname you have for him."

"Wheez, please? Listen."

"Okay. Okay. I'm hearing and listening, not exactly the same things. Ya know?"

Reese walked over to the window again, parted the curtains, and consumed her crush with her eyes. Finally, she turned back to Wheez. "No judging, Wheez. None."

Wheez nodded.

"It's the guy out there. The one in the middle of the block on the other side of the street. The vending table selling purses and music."

In a flash, Wheez had gotten up, snatched up the pair of binoculars, and almost thrust her whole upper half out of the window. "Oooh. Mmm," she moaned. "I see. Him."

Reese pulled her back inside. "Don't, Wheez. Me and you can't be digging on the same dude."

"Well, I can't help it if I'm attracted to rough-around-the-edges boys in fitteds—"

Reese tilted her head. "No, Wheez. He doesn't have on a hat . . ."

Wheez stuck her head back out the window, binoculars pressed against her face. "Well, who then? I know not the one *behind* the table. Not him. *Broke-Up?* Really?"

Reese had her best friend by the shoulders before she knew it. "You know him? Know him, know him?"

"Yeah. Like know him, know him enough to hook you up. I can't believe you don't know who he is . . . his brother goes—"

"I can't believe you didn't tell me about him," Reese said, interrupting Wheez.

Wheez picked up her cell. "He's in my contacts, I buy purses from him. Just say the word, and I'll text or call."

Reese looked at Wheez, biting her lips in thought. She didn't have anyone to produce with. Was totally single now that she'd set Blaze out with the trash. She shrugged. She really had nothing to lose and everything to gain. "The word. But tell him I want to work on some tracks with him. I'll do the rest." She smiled. Her day was turning out better than she thought.

Wheez pressed SEND on her phone. "Done. Now we just wait. Wait and get dressed."

Reese nodded, barely able to contain herself. The orchestra idea may've belonged to Mrs. Allen, but the night was hers. She felt like the star of the concert, and they weren't even there yet. The hottest and flyest chick to grace Central Park. Yes, she could picture it now, her and Broke-Up making history together—music and the A-list couple of the decade. Everything would be perfect, her new, self-confident ego told her. Then her eyes trailed to the vibrating phone in Wheez's hand, and her heart pounded.

Wheez handed the phone to Reese. "Your medicine. Not mine. Don't know if it's good or bad."

Reese selected the text, then opened it. The biggest smile she'd ever grinned stretched her face until she thought it'd split. He'd texted his number, said he'd love to work with her, and wanted them to come to the table. Now.

15

ZIGGY

She was there. *Her*. She stood by his locker with books cradled to her chest, and a wide smile. Ziggy locked eyes with her, and his world paused. He couldn't understand for the life of him what it was about this girl that made her different from the others. But there was something. Throwing on his suave, he bit his bottom lip a bit, tried to look secure, hard around the edges even. He couldn't let her know he was soft on her. There was no way he'd show his hand first. If anyone was going to admit they liked the other, she had to do it first. He had a rep to protect and maintain, and pretty or not, he wasn't going to let her ruin his title.

Her smile widened when he was two steps from her, and he recognized she had deep dimples he hadn't before noticed. She also had the straightest teeth he'd ever seen, and her eyes lit. Everything about her said *I'm the girl for you*. If only he knew her name.

"Ziggy," she said, stepping toward him. "You want to come by my house some time to practice? We have a makeshift studio in the basement with mirrors, a ballet bar, and everything."

He wanted to smile. Grin. Cheese or something, but he didn't. He just gave her a slight head nod. He was a dude, he couldn't show his emotions. No, there would be absolutely no girlin' for him—on the surface, anyway. He was going to play it cool. "Word? When you wanna do that?"

She shrugged. "Whenever. My parents work kinda late, so I was thinking either after school or during our supplemental time . . . if we have the same schedule. It might be best if we were alone. Ya know what I mean?"

They had the same schedule, at least they did or would as far as Ziggy was concerned. He'd skip class to hang out with her at her house, especially alone. He looked at his watch as if his answer was on his wrist, then pressed his lips together in thought. "I think I can swing that. I gotta check on my vending table—I'm an entrepreneur. I own my own business—maybe you can come with me, then we can shoot over to your crib." He searched her eyes for a hint of excitement, interest, something. Heck, he worked for himself, and that should've been impressive.

She nodded. "Okay. Meet me at the front exit for supplemental."

"Cool," Ziggy said aloud, but inside he was screaming: *What's it gonna take to get with you? Do you know who I am? Didn't you just hear me say I'm an entrepreneur?*

"What up, Ziggy?" Wheez, dressed like a hoodlum, stopped and said. She had an apple in her hand and a smirk on her face.

Ziggy nodded. "What up, Wheez? Got any more apples?"

She reached in her pocket, pulled one out, and began to shine it on her shirt.

Ziggy reached over and snatched the apple. "C'mon, Wheez! You're rubbing your germs on my apple." He walked to the water fountain across the hall, and rinsed it under the small stream. Turning around, he did a double take at Wheez. "Why are you dressed like that anyway?"

"Acting. I'm trying out for a part. We're doing *Set It Off*, and I want Latifah's role."

"Oh, you got it. Trust me."

"So you know I hooked up Reese with Broke-Up—"

Before Ziggy knew it, he'd snatched Wheez in the empty room next to the fountain. "Wheez!"

"Hey! If you don't get your hands off me, Z, there's gonna be desks moving up in here. You lost your mind?"

Ziggy let her go, and began to pace. "Wheez! Do you know what you just done?"

Wheez crossed her arms, and looked at him cross-eyed. "Nope!" she said, biting into the apple. "But you're gonna tell me or I'm gonna get into character for real, Z. Then I'm gonna mop you across this floor. Putting your hands on me . . ."

Ziggy hopped up on a desk, and laid it all out for Wheez. It bothered him to share his business, to expose that he'd been living a double life, but he had no choice.

None of his classmates except Rikki knew he had to hide his talent from his family.

Wheez shook her head. "Z, my bad. I'm sorry. I had no idea. I'll fix it, or at least I'll try. And maybe you should consider acting too. You've done a heck of a job of it already, may as well bank you some school credit for it. And another thing, you can get the money for school. You got the money on your finger."

Ziggy looked down at the diamond ring his granddad had willed him, and realized Wheez had a point. It would kill him to do it, but he did have an option.

Wheez's words still rang clear while he watched the busy New Yorkers move in fast-forward haste. Paying attention, he finally realized one thing about the city that he'd never noticed before because he was too busy. All the quick-footed people seemed to be after something and moving at jet speed to get it. Ziggy closed his eyes in the middle of the sidewalk, absorbed the quick energy that whooshed by him in a storm of footsteps, and decided if he wanted everything to be okay, he had to act like it would be. He was going after what he wanted, and he couldn't do any better than that. Choosing determination and positivity, he looked over at *her* as she walked next to him, and wondered if he should ask her name. *Nah*, he thought. Broke-Up would do that for him when he brought her to the table. That way, he wouldn't look so stupid and stuck-up. He didn't want to appear to be so arrogant that he didn't even know her name. They'd danced together, he'd touched her hips, her sweat had blended with his. They were almost a couple, they'd grooved that close.

"Z, what the deal?" Broke-Up asked, smiling, looking from Ziggy to the girl, then back to Ziggy again. As usual, the music was loud. The scent surrounding the table was sweet from burning incense, and two customers were walking away with plastic bags with purses and other items. All good things.

"What's up?" Ziggy looked at Broke-Up, shifting his eyes toward the girl like *Say something*. "We need to stock any more items? You straight on cash? I'm asking 'cause I'm getting ready to get out of dodge for a minute."

Broke-Up shifted his eyes back and forth, clearly not getting Ziggy's hint. "What? What?" he kept whispering.

"Ziggy, we have to go. We don't have much time," she said, looking at her watch.

Broke-Up snatched Ziggy by his sleeve, then bent toward his ear. "Ooh. Time for what, Z? What y'all getting ready to do?"

"Hey. You two. Let me see your vending license."

Ziggy froze. The voice couldn't belong to anyone else but a cop. He looked at Broke-Up, and Broke-Up shrugged his shoulders.

16

JAMAICA-KINCAID

Her parents were coming. They were coming, calling, and looking for her. Jamaica shook her head, gulped her fear, and went into actress mode. How she'd skated through Connecticut and into New York so long without them discovering her secret—her lie—was beyond her. Deep inside though, she had to admit, she knew the time would come when she'd have to face reality and bite the proverbial bullet she knew would be shooting her way. As a teenager, there was no way she could get away with tricking them forever. She was still under their care, hog-tied with their parental power, and she could feel her freedom tick-tocking away. But she wouldn't let them stomp the life out of her acting bug, as she was sure they'd call it. What she had wasn't a bug, common colds were that. She had a real live dream that they couldn't step on and crush.

"Morning, Mother!" Jamaica said, shifting the computer toward the corner of her room that she'd dressed with beautiful fabric the theater no longer needed. She looked behind her, and nodded at the damask-covered stack of milk crates that looked like a high-end table, and was topped off by an equally appealing lamp. From her parents' end, she was sure it looked like she was sitting in the lap of luxury.

"Jamaica. Jamaica?" her mother's voice asked.

And there it was, Jamaica thought. Her mother's face blurred to oblivion, as it popped up on the screen, clearly too close to the camera as usual. She was also loud, which Jamaica expected.

"Oh, technical difficulties again, Brad. We really need to invest in some new equipment," her mom was complaining to her dad.

Jamaica's head rotated side to side. It was really a shame how her mother could never get the Skype thing right. "Good morning, Mother!" she greeted her again, chipper as ever.

"Ahh. There she is, Brad. Do you see her? Good morning, Jamaica. Can you see me? Do you hear me?"

The milky skin, perfect makeup, and huge diamonds were shown on the monitor in such clarity, she almost didn't see her. Her mother's extras shined brighter than she did, but Jamaica saw her. In fact, she looked at her every morning in the mirror, and it bothered her that she was so pretty. Pretty was for puppies and models. Jamaica wanted to be taken serious, be the go-getter like her dad.

"I see you, Mother. How are you? Where are you?" Jamaica had to ask. She'd received the text from her sister this morning that her parents were on their way to Connecticut. She hadn't sent the money Jamaica needed, but she gave information. She couldn't ask for better than that. Well, she reasoned, she couldn't afford better than that because that's exactly what she'd been paying for, according to her sister's message. Somehow they'd agreed to Jamaica paying all of her money to her sister for info, never mind that she needed to eat and get to school. Her sister didn't care about that. *But*, Jamaica shrugged, *that's what little rich girls had a habit of . . . not caring.* But why would they? she questioned. They hadn't a care in the world.

"We're on the plane to see you," her mom yelled into the speakers.

Hunh?! Panic rolled in immediately. "When are you getting th—I mean, here?"

Her dad popped up on the screen now, his face in front of her mother's. "Couple of stops first, darling. I'd say . . ." He turned his back on her, asked someone else, probably one of his assistants she hadn't yet met: "What is our Connecticut ETA?"

She couldn't make out whatever whoever said, but it sounded like a bit too soon for her comfort. "Well, Father, I may not be in Connecticut if it's a weekend. Gully has this thing in New York, and I'm going with. She needs my motivation," she threw out as a hook since her dad was a motivational guru and coach. "Plus, I told her I'd help her and some of the other cast members with makeup from Mom's line." *There, that should do it. Two baits, hooks, and, hopefully, bites.*

Brad moved back in front of the camera, clearly more tech savvy than her mom. "When, darling?"

"I'm sorry, let me look. When did you say you were coming again?" She pretended to scour her calendar— her academic one, where she'd normally write everything down because the boarding school insisted. It was now empty, of course. But it looked good on camera, she was sure.

"Two weekends from now, darling. Mix-up in the schedule, I'm afraid," he said, pronouncing schedule like shedge-dual.

"Nope. No good," Jamaica answered, then flashed her calendar at the screen too fast for anyone to make out.

"Well, we're coming to you. I'd love to see how much you've motivated Gully, and I know Mother would like nothing more than to see how her line works on stage."

She touched her wrist to see if she still had a pulse. She was sure she was going to die, or would very soon from acting malnutrition—a disease her parents would inflict on her once they found her out.

"I have to quit. I know I have to," she said to Mateo as they walked the halls.

Music blasted; people sang, mimed, got into their respective arts as if they were the only ones in the hall. Mateo gave a pound to a few guys, winked at a couple of girls.

"Do you hear me, Teo?" she asked, cutting his name in half.

He stopped, placed both of his hands on her shoulders,

and gave her his full attention. "No, you *don't*. We don't quit—actors *never* quit. We just take on new roles. Life is a production."

"It certainly is. And what's this I hear about your quitting?" Mr. S. asked.

"Okay, now I'm going to die," Jamaica uttered, not sure how Mr. S. had snuck up on them and, more importantly, how she was going to explain. "In the theater now!" he ordered in a serious tone that didn't match his cotton-candy pants and red, black, and green tunic. Jamaica's eyes stretched. Sure enough, Mr. S. had on a Black Power African-inspired tunic, pink slacks, yellow flip-flops, and, to make the color-clashing gods happy, a Jewish yarmulke on his head. And Mr. S. was neither black nor Jewish, but definitely confused, she decided.

In seconds they were in the theater, and Jamaica did her best to explain her situation, leaving out that she was basically half of a runaway because she wasn't totally missing, and that she lived alone. She made it clear that her parents would make her leave Harlem CAPA, and even clearer on it being her dream that she wouldn't— couldn't—give up.

Mr. S. nodded, looked off into the distance, then threw his hands in the air. He stood proud, made his declaration with the top of his lungs: "We act our way through this. That's what we do. Act."

Jamaica looked at him crossways. "Can't you get fired?"

"For what? Teaching you, Jamaica? I'm not sneaking. I'm not lying. And neither are you. You're acting. Your whole stint here has been an act. Your conversation—

lies, all acting. Fix it. Get into character. But you will not quit. Would you like me to talk to them?"

Jamaica took a long look at Mr. S. She knew he meant well, but there was no way she could put him in front of her parents. Not looking the way he always did. They'd think he was base, low—a clown. "Sorry, Mr. S., and no offense, really. But they'd never take you serious . . . not with the way you dress."

He bounded, paced. "I'm an actor, young lady. I can become anything and anyone, including royalty . . . or a Rockefeller who owns a school for artists, but will include leadership studies next semester." He nodded and smiled, pleased with himself.

And Jamaica was just as pleased. "That may work, Mr. S. It may."

17

LA-LA

One hundred and twenty-fifth Street had a life of its own. La-La ascended the subway two stairs at a time, trying to keep up with the others jogging by her. Everyone, not just the street above, was full of energy. La-La looked around as soon as she made it to the landing. Ziggy's vendor's table was to her right and down the block. That's what he'd told her. *Or was it to the left?* She had been so anxious about their meeting that she couldn't remember. All she knew was that she was there, finally, and she'd find him. She could sniff him out anywhere, that's how much she liked him.

"Excuse me, young sistah?" a man said to her, sitting on the dirty ground just inches away from where she stood. He was much older, and the gray hair edging his temples had a yellow hue. Hunched forward a bit, his back had a slight hump on one side, and his face was hardened. La-La could tell that he and life had fought, and he hadn't been the winner. He outstretched a dirty, calloused hand. "Can you spare some money so an old man can eat?"

La-La's heart wrenched. She wanted to reach in her pocket and give the man what she could, but she knew better. She was uptown after all, and in Harlem you couldn't just show your softer side to anybody, especially how much cash was in your pocket. She shrugged and lied: "Sorry."

"That's right, little sistah. Do not give him anything," another older man with a head full of whitish-gray hair said. He offered her his hand. "Sandman's the name, Harlem's my game. You lost?"

La-La shook her head in the negative. "No, I'm good."

Sandman walked up to her, hooking his hands through his striped suspenders. "Good? That's all? You're here. Breathing. If you need your life any better come see me. I can get my hands on happiness—for a price."

La-La took that as her cue to walk. She headed in the direction she hoped Ziggy's table was. Hip-hop rattled her eardrums and the storefront window behind her as a SUV bellowed by, blasting music. La-La nodded to the rhythm, humming low. She didn't recognize the song, but the beat was hot. And so was the sun, she realized as a streak of sweat slid down her face.

"La-La," a voice she didn't recognize called out from behind with a heavy West Indian accent.

Turning slowly, she was cautious. The voice didn't belong to Ziggy, that she was sure. She'd memorized his with her heart because every time she heard it, it crumbled her self-assuredness and made her stumble on her words.

"Hey!" Ziggy yelled, waving his arms as if he was helping a plane land. "Over here, pretty gal!"

La-La locked eyes with him, smiled, and waved. She perked up, almost dancing her way down the street.

"This ya gal then, Star?" a guy standing next to Ziggy, wearing a ragged and clearly bootleg vending license around his neck, asked as La-La reached the vending table. He was a bit taller than Ziggy, but La-La could tell they were definitely cut from the same cloth. They were mirror images.

Ziggy smiled, and slightly threw his head back like he was saying what's up. "That's La-La, my future wifey." He elbowed the guy. "La-La, say hello to my brother, Broke-Up," he said, pronouncing his brother's name brock-up.

She drew her eyebrows together, sure she had heard him wrong. "Hunh? Did you just call him Broke-Up, as in broke up, or Brock something?

Ziggy and his brother laughed. Ziggy placed his arm around his almost-twin, his eyes lit up like a Fourth of July night sky. "Yes, this is my brother. We call him Broke-Up."

Broke-Up stuck out his leg, then pointed to his knee. "My leg's got pins in it, 'olding it together. And my family takes it for a joke. They don't care what I think. Rude people. See?" he said.

La-La smiled. "So, I should call you . . . ?"

Broke-Up's laugh cut through the air in a pitch higher than she'd ever heard a guy reach, and she couldn't help but smile harder.

Ziggy walked around the vending table, took her hand in his, kissed her on the cheek, and owned her. He made her shudder. "That's another reason we call him Broke-Up—'cause his laugh will break up anything."

Broke-Up sucked his teeth. "Let's hope it'll break up five-ohs attention if they catch us with this homemade license again. And you be careful there, La-La. My pitch might break up things, but Ziggy here, he breaks young gals hearts. Man has *no* respect for the sweet. None."

He held her hand. Wouldn't let it go, no matter where they went or who saw them. La-La couldn't believe how much of a gentleman Ziggy was. He'd treated her to lunch, took her to the dance store and showed her a pair of shoes he'd been saving for. He'd even taken her around his friends, then paid for a cab to take them to Greenwich Village where he showed her a couple of other spots she could sing at; then they trained it to Midtown. Now she sat next to him, feeling on top of the world despite her problems with Nakeeda and wanting to erase Remi's illness.

"I can't remember the last time I had so much fun hanging out with a girl. You think you're gonna check out Café Wha and The Village Underground? I think you could really blow at both—it's no telling who'll be scouting for talent."

La-La nodded her answer, then closed her eyes and

gripped the balled-up paper that had housed the hero sandwich Ziggy'd made her eat hours after lunch. She welcomed the breath of wind that breezed and Ziggy's companionship. Leaning back against the Central Park bench, she smiled. Ziggy couldn't have come into her life at a better time—she needed a positive spin on her reality, and some braces would be nice. And the things he'd put her up on since hanging out with him could definitely help her wrap some tracks around her teeth. *I'll get them. In due time.* A smile threatened to spread across her face. A lurking, sure grin she'd been void of for months. She *would* get what she wanted. Period. She didn't know when, but she knew how. She'd sing in the Village and on subway platforms.

Ziggy's hand was playing in her hair before she knew it. "Why you smiling?" he asked when La-La opened her lids, peering up at him.

His eyes asked so much more than his words. His eyes bore into her. Made her shift in her seat. She wasn't sure what was hiding behind his look, but something was. *Pity? Empathy? No. Attraction. Yes, he's definitely feeling me more than before.* She shrugged her shoulders in answer to his question, then looked at him intensely. "Why're you hawking me like that, Ziggy?"

His fingers continued to dance in her hair. Scooting closer, he leaned into her. Kept looking into her eyes. Didn't stop playing with her hair. "I'm just checking out your shirt. It's hot."

"Think so?" La-La smiled. She was going to scoot away, but killed the thought and closed her eyes again.

Enjoyed Ziggy's closeness. She felt safe with him. And something else. She was really digging him, not just wrapped up in his good looks and charm.

Wait! Her inquisitiveness plagued her. She had to ask. Had to question the stereotype. After all, Ziggy *was* a male dancer. Was it possible that he was being brother-friendly to her and concealing a secret with his womanizing ways? Without further thought, she sat up, searched his eyes for truth. "No disrespect, Ziggy. But I gotta know something. Is it cool to be open with you?"

Ziggy nodded. Smiled as if he already knew what La-La would ask.

La-La fidgeted. "Well, you are a dancer. . . ." She stopped, didn't know how to tactfully ask.

Ziggy laughed. "And you wanna know if I'm gay or bisexual, right?"

La-La nodded.

"It's cool," Ziggy assured her. "I'm used to it. But to answer your question . . ." He glided his palm across her cheek, causing tingles to rush through her. "I'm try-everything. I'll try anything once, twice if I like it . . . but only with girls. Somethin' you wanna try with me?" He teased, then grabbed the balled-up paper from her hand and pulled her up from the bench. "Come on. Let me show you how dancers do it—super-straight dancers who may just have a thing for you. If you lose, you sing in the Village tomorrow night!"

La-La wiggled her non-hips as she thrust her butt higher in the air. Bent over, her fingertips touched the grass, and one of Ziggy's palms rested on her lower back while the other dangled between her parted thighs.

I could get used to this. She inhaled her emotions, enjoyed the heat radiating from Ziggy's body and the descending sun. In only hours, she'd discovered he was magnificent. Talented. Smart. Considerate in his own way, he was just what she needed. A positive new beginning at Harlem CAPA. Turning only her head to look at him, she maintained her position. Rocked ever so slightly to lure and bait. Her infatuated eyes confirmed what she'd already known. *Beautiful. If he were candy,* he'd *be my favorite flavor.* Ziggy was magnetic. She decided right then and there, bent over with him gripping her hips, she was just the magnet to stick to him.

"You're supposed to say hut one, hut two. Hut. Hut," Ziggy urged.

La-La grasped the balled-up paper, said her hut-huts, then passed it between her legs into Ziggy's awaiting hand. Stumbling backward, she laughed. Couldn't remember the last time she'd felt so comfortable or had had so much fun. How two people could play football, she didn't know. But she sure was going to hang with him long enough to find out. *Just for today,* she promised herself. It wasn't against anybody's law for her to be happy for a few hours before she had to return to the dramatic Boom-Keshas and Nakeedas of the world. But for now, she'd enjoy Ziggy. See what he had to offer her.

"Run out for the pass, baby," Ziggy yelled, holding up the balled paper, assuming a quarterback's stance.

Baby? echoed in her mind as she ran out, awkwardly

turned to receive his throw, and then, "Oh, shii—Sugar. Honey. Iced. Tea," La-La mumbled, catching the curse but not her balance. Her butt kissed the ground before she knew it. Arms flailed. Toes pointed to the sky. Legs split into a V. Defeated, La-La lay her head on the grass. She couldn't believe she'd busted her behind in front of the dude she was trying to impress. And to top it all off, she'd lost.

"You a'ight?" Ziggy stood over her, extending his hand to help her up.

"Yeah, I'm good," La-La answered, accepting his hand, and laughing away her embarrassment.

The corners of Ziggy's mouth tugged into a smile. "I've never seen nobody bust their butt so elegantly. You *should* be a dancer . . . or maybe stick to singing since you'll be doing that tomorrow night," he teased.

"Oh, you got jokes!"

"That's not all I got, La-La. Believe it!" Ziggy shot back, lacing his arm through hers.

"Oh, I *do* believe it. And I also believe you owe me"— her wanting eyes drank him in—"*something* to quench my thirst."

Ziggy reared back his head in laughter. "I got you, baby. I know just what you need."

"Bet you do," La-La flirted, walking next to him.

For a moment she floated. Swore her feet lifted and the air licked the bottoms of her shoes. She'd never felt so light before. Was sure she was experiencing the natural high she'd once heard about. Yes, she could get used to this, she thought. She loved being with Ziggy. Enjoyed how he'd zoomed in on her, making her feel like the center of his world.

"I do," he said, stopping and turning to her. He grabbed her cheeks in his hands, then changed her world with her first kiss.

18

REESE

The halls were dark. Dreary. Empty. Welcoming. Reese tipped down the hall, careful not to let her sneakers squeak. She looked behind her, held her finger to her mouth, letting Broke-Up know to keep it down. His feet were heavy. Well, maybe just one foot. The one attached to the leg that had pins in it that kept popping when he walked. She smiled, unsure if she should believe him or not. Was it really possible for someone to have their legs held together by pins? Or was it a joke?

A loud crash sounded down the hall, making Reese cringe.

"Who's that?" Broke-Up asked, whispering as loud as his knee was cracking.

And there he was. Half-Dead. Lying on the floor, holding his knee, rolling from side to side, claiming he was okay. Reese walked up to him, put her hands on her hips, and looked down at him, her head rotating the entire time. What was he doing in the school after hours anyway? She was almost afraid to ask, but had to.

"Half-Dead? Why are you here? What were you doing?"

"Ay, what's up, Reese?" he asked, still holding his knee.

She drew her eyebrows together, tapped her foot. "Well?"

Broke-Up helped Half-Dead up from the floor. "Man, I understand. My knee is no good too. None."

Reese looked at her two broken friends who only had two good feet between their four.

"The doctor said there was a possibility that I would get the feeling back in half of my foot. So I was trying to perfect that dance move. The one I'm not able to master yet."

She tsked him. "You mean the one you'll never be able to master? Half-Dead, no offense, but without feeling in half of your foot—your toes, especially—you can't spin on them. Stop it with the ballet moves. Sing or something."

Half-Dead looked surprised. He glanced at Broke-Up. "See? See how they do me around here? You'd think they'd give me some credit for trying."

Broke-Up laughed. "Nah, Star. I can't run with you on this one. My knee's held together with pins, so I don't play sports. If half of your foot is dead, why dance? Dudes shouldn't twinkle toe anyway. Feel me?"

Reese walked away from that comment, wondering if Broke-Up was really that deluded. Men danced. Real bona fide, hard-legged, women-having men. Talking loud as if it were okay for them to be in the school after hours, they followed behind her, conversing the whole time.

She shushed them. "We're not supposed to be here. Quiet." She stopped, peeked inside of the music room, and saw it was empty. Carefully, she pushed open the door, directed the two to hold each other up so they wouldn't run into anything.

"Where we going, Reese?" Half-Dead asked, skipping, apparently afraid to put weight on his banged-up knee and half-numb foot. He flipped on the lights, then stared at Broke-Up. "You know you look exactly like this dude that goes here. A dancer!" he laughed.

Reese ran, then shut off the lights. "Okay, Half-Dead, it's been nice. But we need to work."

He hobbled over to the light switch, bouncing up and down in place on his good foot, and looked from Reese to Broke-Up. "What kinda work *we* need to do in the music room?"

"Make beats. I gots that bass line she—"

"Half-Dead, please? I'm serious. Nothing you need to know about."

Still hopping, he shook his head. "Nothing I need to know about or *tell* about?"

Broke-Up stepped up now. "You a snitch?"

"All right. All right. Dang!" He grabbed his bag, and literally bounced out of there.

Reese stood behind the boards, amazed at Broke-Up's familiarity with the equipment. They had full access to a forty-eight track SSL control board, one of the best boards on the market, and she couldn't have been prouder of what they were coming up with. She was comfortable with Broke-Up, loved his vibe. And his ear? Wow, his ear for music was phenomenal. Their heads nodded in sync with the drums. They both hummed, almost beat boxed with the fire beats blazing out of the speakers. It was if they'd always been a team, as if there had never been a Blaze in her life—in her way. She looked over at Broke-Up, and loved that he was as moved as she. That was why he was there. That's why she'd have chosen him over Blaze if she had to pick. He was as much in love with producing as she was, and his sound was his testimony.

"This is hot," she exclaimed, wrapping him in her embrace. She squeezed him with all her might, more excited than she'd been in a long time.

His arms were wrapped around her before she knew it, and neither seemed to want to pull away. So she stayed there. Stayed as long as she could, inhaling the music with her pores and his scent with her nose. She wasn't sure if it was from vending on One-two-five or not, but he smelled like every perfumed oil in existence that reeked deliciousness.

Broke-Up finally broke the hold. "You know if we keep doing this, we're gonna make more than music? I'm not a twinkle toes like your boy Half-Dead."

Reese didn't know whether to smile or defend Half-Dead. "Don't call him twinkle toes, please. And . . . what's so wrong with us making more than music? I thought it'd be nice to make something like history *together*."

He looked at her and bit his bottom lip. "We can make a lot of things together, beginning and ending with this." He grabbed her face in his hands, and gave her a kiss on the forehead. "Now." He let her go and turned back to the boards. "Let's get it done. We got a party coming up where we can pass out demos, and maybe we can sell some of these beats."

Reese shrugged, and swallowed her excitement of the kiss. "Cool. You know this is a performing arts school. We can also get some writers, and there's this fab singer La-La we can have reference the tracks," she added.

19

ZIGGY

Ziggy's heels thumped against the cement stoop as he sat swinging his feet and contemplating. For the first time in a long while he felt he had options. Two problem solvers that ranged from bad to worse. Still, he had possibilities. Pawn the ring or face his worst nightmare: leaving performing arts school. As he rubbed his hand over his head, Ziggy's mind went numb. He'd been trying get the guts to give up the ring since Wheez had broached him with the idea. But how was he to decide between losing two things he loved and wanted to keep more than anything, his dancing and his grandfather's gift? Sure, he could dance better than any of the dudes he'd seen on television, but he wasn't there yet. And the competition was too far away for him to factor in prize money. *And the vending table isn't doing well because it's a recession. It's too hard out here for people to waste money on boot-*

leg stuff. And we gotta keep moving it to avoid five-oh because we got a homemade license. It's too hard out here. . . .

Sucking his teeth in aggravation, he hopped off the stoop and stomped his foot. He was sick of it all. His entire situation was butt backwards and wearing him thin. Digging into his pocket, he retrieved the advertisement for the pawnshop that he'd torn out of the phone book, then quickly put it back. He wasn't ready to make the decision, not now. First he'd go upstairs and sleep on it, that's what he'd do. That's what his father did when something heavy was on his mind. His mother too. She prayed, slept, and swore she woke up with an answer.

Before his key plunged into the lock, Ziggy knew two things. Sleep was out of the question and there was a problem. A piece of paper taped to the painted brown door read FAMILY MEETING FRIDAY @ 7 P.M.! BE HERE OR MOVE. Ziggy reread the note, shook his head. All caps in Sharpie topped off with a threat. Trouble had definitely risen, and he hoped it wasn't him, but, somehow, knew it was. Ziggy searched his mind, wondered what happened, what he could've possibly done, but couldn't think of a thing. Maybe, just maybe, it was Broke-Up, he thought. Then changed his mind.

"Great." He exhaled and simultaneously slid the key into the lock, prepared to find out the problem sooner than later. Today was his father's day off. *Probably Dad's day to go off,* Ziggy worried. "Last thing I need is to be on Pop's list," he mumbled, opening the door and sucking in his breath until his stomach swelled. Readied for his dad's rant, Ziggy was caught off guard. There was no fussing or I-told-you-sos, just sunshine, ancient reggae music, and a welcoming aroma he hadn't smelled since forever. *Oxtails?*

Shhh. Shuffle. Slap. Shhh. Shuffle. Slap. The sound repeated, growing in loudness as slippered feet shuffled toward him. *Ma*, Ziggy mused, a grin lifted the corners of his mouth as he thought about his mother and the house slippers she wore religiously, and wondered if he'd ever seen his mother's feet.

"Afternoon, baby," Ma greeted with a dishrag in her hand and an apron wrapped around her waist.

"Hey, Ma." Ziggy bent over and kissed his mother's soft cheek. "I seen Pop's note on the door. What I do this time?"

Ma chuckled, waved away Ziggy's words, and beckoned him into the kitchen. "Don't mind him. He was born on a full moon—wild as tidal waves, angry as the night waters."

"Well, what's his problem then?" Ziggy asked, setting his book bag on the counter. Lifting a lid off a pot and picking up a long-handled spoon, he waited for the steam to clear so he could sample the oxtails.

"Scat," Ma chastised, snatching the spoon from Ziggy. "Ya know better than to be messing with my pots. Your pop's mad at the world for the same reason as always, I reckon. And that'd be no reason a'tall."

Ziggy released his weight onto a kitchen chair at the small table, then toyed with the salt and pepper shakers and his indecision about the ring and school—and living in a house where he couldn't dream or dance. He'd thought about leaving plenty of times, but he was too young and couldn't afford it. Yet. He couldn't take too much more of his father's emotions which swung back and forth between hate and hate more while Ziggy's bounced between afraid to be himself and resentment. Theirs had become a silent battle of son versus father.

"Ma, I can't take this no more," Ziggy said, his words more of a plea than a statement. "Pop is just too hard on us because we're boys. And I'm tired. . . . I work, go to school, help around here."

Ma stopped stirring the oxtail, and turned to Ziggy. "Your dad is just being your dad, baby. He's always been that-a-way. . . ."

"Been what way?" his dad's voice boomed from the kitchen doorway.

Ziggy almost jumped out of his skin, he was so scared. Not afraid of his father—not totally, he just hadn't heard him come in. He looked at his dad, then saw Broke-Up appear behind him.

"What the deal with this note, Pop?" Broke-Up asked, walking around their father and heading straight toward their mom. He kissed her cheek. "We're all here now. Put it on the table."

Ziggy stood silent.

His mother turned off the stove, then excused herself with: "Man's business, this is. Call me when you finish."

Broke-Up raised his brows, waiting.

Their father pulled out a chair, turned it around backward, then straddled it. He looked at them both like he could kill them, as if he would.

Ziggy shook his head. He couldn't understand how someone could bring children into the world yet manage to always find some reason to threaten them. How could you look at a miniature version of yourself and not feel love?

Pop sucked his teeth, a habit the whole family had. He looked at Broke-Up, then over to Ziggy. "Now one of you tell me which one of you's a batty boy?" he asked, using a West Indian derogatory word for gay male.

Without thought the brothers exchanged glances and said, "Hunh?"

Broke-Up broke out in their native tongue, clearly offended. "What'cha talk 'bout, batty boy? No batty boys 'ere."

Ziggy shook his head. "We like women. Girls. Thick thighs and smooth skin. Ain't nobody want no man. You crazy?" Anger fueled his words.

Pop nodded, stood up, then slid the chair back to the table. "Okay. That's what I thought. Sandman and his drunk friends lying on my boys then, talkin' 'bout one of yous dancing. I told them that it couldn't be my boys—not living under this roof. No dancers can live here!"

Ziggy's heart dropped to his dance shoes, but his face didn't show it.

Broke-Up laughed. "Pop, stop listening to your drunk friends in the street. They just jealous 'cause your boys are making it happen." Then his face turned serious, and he gave Ziggy his full attention. "Besides, me and Z don't have time for that batty-boy mess or the rumors. We gotta get money. The cops took our vending license and confiscated our merchandise."

Ziggy would've cried if he was alone.

20

JAMAICA-KINCAID

Jamaica was sure someone had stabbed her pupils with an ice pick. A burning heat blinded and assaulted her eyes, traveled through her sockets, and rocked her brain. Her head was going to combust, and cerebellum would explode in any second. The blare of the morning sun had come with a headache. Cradling her skull, Jamaica tried to speak, but a dry stickiness wouldn't allow her to. Dirty, dry cotton had to be moister than her mouth. Squeezing shut her eyes, she cupped her hands in front of her lips and blew into them. Hot breath returned.

"*Ill,*" she whispered, cringing from the awful smell. "Dragon breath." *Never again,* she thought, wondering if this is what people meant by feeling like they had a hangover. She almost shook her head, but was afraid to. She was certain that whatever feeling hungover was like, she had awoken with worse. Much worse. Aftereffects from the caffeinated energy drinks she'd guzzled made her feel like her skull was vomiting her brain.

Rolling over onto her side, she froze, searching for an answer. *Where* was she? And why was she still in her clothes? She shut her eyes, tried to think. She'd gone to the party, hung out, networked, drank an energy drink. Or two. Or three. Was escorted out by someone who decided that she was too young to be in the party, then went to her apartment. Or so she believed.

No!

Her temples still pulsed. Throbbed. Banged while she thought.

Home?

That couldn't be right because she definitely wasn't in her room or on her makeshift bed she'd made out of stacking comforters. Or alone, she discovered when the silhouette of someone's body wriggled under the sheet next to her, then went ballistic. *Whoever* was convulsing, and Jamaica scooted away until her back kissed the headboard. She pulled her knees to her chest, held them until they stopped shaking. Afraid to move, she breathed as silently as she could, and watched as the person punched, kicked, squirmed, then calmed. Finally toes shot out from under the sheet. A male's foot. Jamaica smiled knowingly. *Mateo.* She could recognize his beautiful-for-a-boy's toes anywhere. "He's having a nightmare," she whispered, reaching to shake him awake, then decided against it.

The sun's overpowering ray penetrated the light-gray fabric that covered him, and illuminated the outline of his face. He glowed, looked angelic. She curled her index finger, hooked it into his natural curls that peeked from beneath the cover, and played with his hair until he stirred. Relaxing a little, Jamaica unfolded her legs, slid under the sheet next to him, then kicked him with all her might.

"*Ay*," he screamed like a girl, then gave her a half smile. Tiredness was still on his face, and he was fully clothed too, except for his bare feet.

"Morning. Afternoon. Whatever," Jamaica returned the greet. She still played with his hair. "When did I get here? How did I get here? You know you should've been a girl with all of this pretty hair."

Mateo playfully punched her, then shrugged. "*Shud*-dup. *You* should've been a Rasta with your locks." They both laughed. "*Serious*ly though, yo. I don't even remember when or how *I* got here, and I'm supposed to know when *you* did? Get outta here." He pushed her hand away, scratched his head. Sat up with a start. "Wait a minute. . . ." He yawned, stretched. Thought. "Oh, yeah. I ran into you out*side* of the party. I was talking to this bangin' chick, and you was with some dude. Ari . . . something."

"Ari!" Jamaica sat up, smiled. "Ari. You know . . . Ari. *Ari*? *The* agent of agents?! Producer too. He's loaded. Lots of money and power."

"Say *word*?" Mateo asked, nodding his head and waiting for confirmation. "That was *him* . . . the agent slash producer that I hear my mom and Mr. S. talking about? Good stuff," he praised, nodding. "So *what* jumped off? He gonna hook you or what?"

Jamaica jumped up, her words and actions animated. Last night's happenings spilled from her mouth like water. She'd survived the party, the phoniness. The other actors who acted as if the parts they had were meaningless, parts that she'd always dreamed of. But, somehow, she'd done it. She'd sucked up her pride, gone over to Ari, and asked for a chance to audition for him. She'd told him she needed an agent, and he couldn't live without her on his roster. She was going to his office. An agent's office! Today.

"I gotta go," she explained, hopping out of the bed, stumbling, and almost falling. She ran, zigzagging across, then around the room, gathering her shoes and purse as she went. "I gotta meet Ari later. Can't go looking like this."

"*Wait!* " Mateo said, rolling out of bed, and halting her in her tracks.

"Oh yeah, that's right," Jamaica dropped her voice to above a whisper and her butt on the bed. "Think your mom's still here? We're like brother and sister, so it shouldn't matter." She looked up, drew her eyebrows together.

"Nah. *Nah.* She's at her dude's crib. And besides, we *don't* do that brother-sister thing here in the hood. Boys and girls don't sleep together unless they're *sleeping* together. That's that rich-people *stuff* . . . letting the opposite sex spend the night. I told you to wait for *this.*" He grabbed her by her shoulders and pecked her on the lips in a brotherly way. "Good luck. You got *this*, Jamaica. Don't worry. Just *act* like you do!" he smiled.

Jamaica pulled away, hustled over to the bedroom

door. "*Ill!*" She wiped her mouth with the back of her hand. "You got the Dragon too." She paused in the doorway, smiled as she watched Mateo cup, then blow into his hands, and rear his head back from the smell as she had done earlier. "Told you!"

"*Wait!*"

Now Mateo was playing with her, and she didn't have time for it. "What? You know I gotta get ready—"

"Yo, you *forgot* you gotta work a play today?" He looked at the clock, ran his hand through his curls. "Better beat feet. You *only* got a little over an hour."

Jamaica stomped her foot, almost breaking the heel off the stiletto. She didn't have time to change clothes or anything else. She had to get to the theater, and then to see Ari. "I can't let him see me in the same clothes. Gimme something to wear."

Mateo gave her a button-down, a straw Panama Jack hat, and a tie.

Jamaica looked at herself in the mirror. She cuffed the sleeves of the shirt, and left it unbuttoned, but tied the bottom around her waist. She hung the tie around her neck, and topped herself off with the hat. *Not too shabby,* she thought, admiring the look of Mateo's clothes with her dress and stilettos. It was different, but so was she.

Jamaica couldn't keep her eyes off the clock. She'd just gotten there, and couldn't leave fast enough. Sure, it was a paying gig, but not the one she wanted. Not after meeting Ari last night. She cut her eyes low, looked over in the corner where her book bag sat alongside high-paid actresses' Pradas, Guccis, Louis, and Berkins. With temples throbbing over the background rock 'n' roll, Jamaica worked all her stagehand positions before the music stopped and rehearsal began. She floated into one lowly job, out of it, and into the next. This—being a stage slave—she could do with her eyes closed. Help with the props. Run around to help the actors. Be the producers' puppet. She was acting like she liked it, and was good. Forget what Maritzio had thought of her weeks ago, she was great when she wanted to be, and knew it. Her problem was that on most days she just didn't believe it enough.

Today's play was based on underwear. *Hooray for panties*, she tried to pep up after the music ceased and rehearsal began. She tried to find excitement as she watched the thong riding up the crack of the snobby actress's behind. But, try as she might, she couldn't convince herself that the overpriced, silky barely-there panties didn't hurt the poor woman. Every time the lady moved, Jamaica saw them cutting into her circulation and skin. The G-string was razor-blade thin.

"Really?!" the actress yelled, walking off the set, simultaneously stepping out of the panties as if she were alone in a dressing room. "These hurt. I mean really freakin' hurt. They're cutting me," she announced, bending over and spreading her cheeks so Jamaica and the wardrobe ladies could inspect. "See, right there." She pointed, not the least bit shy.

"Put the f'n panties back on! Or find another pair," some lady said in a nasal voice behind Jamaica's back.

Hands clapped, then fingers snapped. "Somebody tell me who this chick is . . . walking off the set like this. She is ridiculous. Disgraceful."

Jamaica whispered to the actress. "Don't do this. Do you know who you're messing with?"

The actress sneered at Jamaica, strutted across the stage, and picked up the panties from the floor. "You wear them then . . . since you know so much. I guess you want to be an actress too. Hunh, wannabe?"

Jamaica ducked the pair of worn underwear, and mumbled. "I can act your part in my sleep."

"Well, do it. Yes, do it. You, there. Yes, you. Silly girl. Show her how."

Jamaica turned, only glimpsed a snatch of the woman's back through a crowd who surrounded her. Tilting her head, Jamaica realized this mysterious woman was talking to her. "'Silly girl'?" Jamaica accidentally snapped, then realized her mistake. Stagehand or not, she was still a person who had feelings. She only hoped she caught herself in time.

Like the Red Sea, the crowd magically parted.

Jamaica froze.

The woman parted her lips, sneered her version of a smile.

Jamaica opened her mouth to speak. To apologize. Explain. Something. *Any*thing. But she couldn't find words. They'd fled right along with her previous attitude. It was the woman's beauty that stopped her, then her minimal stature. Jamaica had heard enough about the lady to know who she was without a formal introduction. The crowd that had split into a V on either side of her, with her in the middle, served as proof enough. Together, they resembled a flock of birds flying south. The woman, Talia, was the head bird in charge.

Talia walked toward Jamaica, then around her, inspecting with crossed arms. She shook her head, slid her Versace rims down her slim nose, and looked her up and down, then up again. After rolling her eyes, she pursed her lips, then smacked out clipped words. "Do it. Show Ms. Diva here how it's done."

Jamaica didn't know what to do. She didn't know if she were in trouble or not. But she was smart enough to know that the woman wasn't playing. She nodded. "Can I have a different pair of panties?"

Talia laughed. "No. No panties needed. I just want you to show the diva how it's done. Humility, you know? You're here to help, stagehand. So help us on the stage . . . if you want your job."

Jamaica gulped. She couldn't lose her job. No way. She didn't care if she failed or embarrassed herself, she had to do it. Especially if she ever wanted to work in New York again. Talia didn't begin with a T or any other letter of the alphabet, Talia began with power. Jamaica closed her eyes, took deep breaths, then became the character. She strutted across the stage babbling about underwear, repeating the actress's lines word for word.

Talia threw up her hands, bounded toward Jamaica, then pulled her inches from her face. "What's your name?"

Jamaica told her.

"Who's your agent, Jamaica?"

"Ari," she lied, using only Ari's first name because that's all she needed. Everyone who was anyone knew who he was.

Talia turned one hundred and eighty degrees, her hands still on Jamaica's collar. "Clear the stage, and you," she said, pointing at the actress who was allergic to the little panties. "You can go home. You've been replaced . . . by the stagehand—the wannabe with the fabulous style."

Tears sprang from Jamaica's eyes. "Really?"

Talia turned back to her, and looked her dead in her eyes without a trace of laughter on her face. "Really. Somebody get me Ari. We've got contracts to sign. And get Ms. Jamaica some ointment and a pair of black boy shorts. All you other girls take a long lunch. I'll see you back here in two hours to the minute. And Jamaica," she said, waving her toddler-size finger in the air. "Don't disappoint me. You have to own this part or we'll both look like fools. Me? Can you imagine . . . hiring a stage hand? And, honey, I hope like hell you can cry as fast as you did just now. That'd be delightful. An actress who can act for once."

Jamaica slid out of her getup and into the boy shorts, worried about the time and lying about Ari. She needed to get to the phone and warn him. She guessed he couldn't be mad now or turn her down. She'd gotten herself a part, and he'd still get agent's commission. Everything would be fine, she told herself, then cringed and wanted to faint when she heard Talia say, "Get Maritzio on the phone. Tell him to cancel all plans he has for the day of the next rehearsal. I have a gift for him."

Worried or not, Jamaica smiled. Who cared what Maritzio used to think? Talia was the head bird in charge. New York was going to be better for her than she'd imagined.

21

LA-LA

"You sure this is the right place for a swimming suit?" La-La asked.

Rikki nodded, then playfully rolled her eyes. "Trust. And maybe a camisole or corset for your performance tonight. We're gonna need all the help we can get to make you look old enough to get in."

A sultry rainbow of silk, lace, push-up bras, and slinky lingerie greeted them when they entered What's-Her-Name's Secret's trendy establishment. La-La couldn't help but finger the too-cute fabrics, furry high-heeled slippers, and attached garters. Ninety-million A through DD cups splashed one section, and coordinating undies, purposely displayed nearby, lured one to buy matching pieces. And La-La took the bait, pulling Rikki along as she eyed one panty, then another, confused. They all looked the same to her. Except for the rare regular cut that wasn't large by her standards.

"They all look the same to you?" she whispered the question to Rikki.

"Don't tell me you've never been here either," Rikki answered in disbelief. "First Cyd—can't believe she refused to come in here and thinks this is a hooker-clothing store—and now you're just as green as her. Good thing you two met me!"

La-La looked around the store. "I never needed to come here. I'm in ninth grade, remember? I buy *comfortable* panties."

"You're kidding, right? They are comfy, most of 'em. Feel 'em and see."

La-La reached for a pretty blue pair, and before she could touch them a saleslady attacked her.

"Can I help you find something in particular? A certain cut?"

"Cut?" La-La asked. "No. We're just looking. I'll let you know if I need help."

Saleslady smiled and eyed her. Ignored her put-off. "Yes, cut. We have French cut. Brazilian. G-strings. Thongs. Low-ride bikinis. Crotchless—no, never mind. You won't be needing the crotchless, now, will you?"

Who knew there were so many different kinds of panties? La-La looked at Rikki. Maybe she knew the difference because La-La surely didn't. Did French women and Brazilian women wear different kinds of underwear? If so, didn't someone make American panties for American women? It couldn't be possible that panties were assigned by nationality. She came close to asking Saleslady what if she were half French, born in South America, but raised in California? What kind of panty would she be assigned then?

Rikki must've read the confusion on her face. "Regular bikinis please, with matching bras. Somethin' lacy," she said matter-of-factly.

"Something racy," La-La added for effect, in hopes of irritating Saleslady, who'd been looking down on them as if they were children, not young adults.

"Who knows, maybe even the crotchless . . . breathing would be nice," Rikki added, catching on to the game.

They followed Saleslady through the maze of lingerie. Every couple of steps, she paused, cleared her throat, and La-La would smile. She'd discovered a way to piss her off; she touched the garments on every rack that they passed, leaving a trail of swinging hangers.

La-La stopped, finding the perfect pair. Lime-green and lacy, the pair looked more like bikini bottoms. Something she could live with. Removing the panties from the rack, she held them in front of her pants. Then looked at the price tag. "Thirty dollars? Thirty freakin' dollars? For a pair of panties? What, is the bra free?" La-La flipped out at the top of her lungs despite Rikki shushing her. She couldn't believe What's-Her-Name's Secret was charging that much for a flimsy piece of material that rode up the butt by design. There was no way she was going to pay that much for a crotch-cover with a string.

"What's your budget?" Saleslady asked, clearly rattled.

"Budget?" Rikki answered for La-La.

"Yes." Saleslady forced a smile through gritted teeth.

"Because there are a couple of other stores that may have something else. You know, something within your price range."

"She's good," Rikki said to Saleslady, then turned to La-La. Gave her just the fuel she needed. "Ziggy will love them. They look just like swimsuit bikini bottoms—no one else will stand out like you."

La-La gave Saleslady the once-over, swinging the lime bikinis, her adrenaline feeding her with each sway of the panties. "You shouldn't judge books by covers. That's cliché. Just like your attitude. So what if we don't *look* like we can afford these? In one week I made over a thousand dollars on the Market," she lied. "You know, Wall Street? How much did you pull in from selling butt riders and tit lifters?" La-La spat, checking Saleslady's attitude. She was there to find something to disguise her flats that would help reel in Ziggy. Not make friends. La-La snatched a bra in her size off an adjoining rack. "Show us to the dressing room. *Please.*"

La-La slid the bikinis over her cotton briefs, and admired herself in the mirror. They did look good. *Much better than these semi-parachutes.*

"Got something sexy?" Cyd's question blared through the fitting room door.

"Oh, so you came anyway. Did you find some guts or buy some? Thought you didn't like lingerie stores," La-La said, cracking open the door and poking her head out. "Come tell me what you two think?"

Cyd looked around, then slid into the fitting room

with Rikki on her heels. "I said I didn't like hooker stores. Most of these are just fronts for some illegal stuff."

La-La and Rikki ignored Cyd. "The color looks good on you," Rikki complimented, holding up a black corset with detachable spaghetti straps. "You like this? This is what you're wearing tonight. It's grown and sexy, and we can fill the cups to give you some ta-tas."

Broke-Up patted her on the back like a proud brother-in-law as she prepared to go on the tiny stage. "You're gonna do well, La-La. I just know it."

La-La looked at him and smiled. She'd had no idea he was an upcoming music producer and DJ or that he had so much pull in adult clubs. But she was glad he did. If it weren't for him and Ziggy, she'd be relegated only to train stations. *Money is money*, she reminded herself.

An extra pair of hands were touching her arm. She looked to her right, and locked eyes with Ziggy. "A kiss for luck?" he asked.

Rikki stood next to him sticking out her tongue.

"Go kill it, La-La," Cyd yelled, giving her a thumbs-up.

La-La smiled at them all, then nodded her yes to Ziggy, and just like that—he sparked magic in her.

La-La stepped on stage proud and tall, and borrowed the magic Ziggy had given her to bring the crowd to tears. She ended with: "Thank you. That was for Remi."

22

REESE

Reese eased through the crowded industry party with Wheez next to her with her mouth hung open, ogling all the celebrities. Reese elbowed her, and whispered for her to stop acting so green. It was bad enough they were too young to be there, and had dressed sexier than usual to appear older, she didn't want to risk standing out because of it, and get booted in front of everyone. No, she couldn't handle or afford that type of embarrassment, not when she had networking to do and CDs to pass out. She was here to make connects, not industry friends, and she'd told Wheez that before they'd got there. Standing on tiptoe, she looked for Broke-Up. He'd hooked them up with passes, and told her he'd be there. But where was he? she wondered, not seeing him anywhere.

"Woo-hoo," Wheez called out to someone. She reared back her head, laughed, and acted very Hollywood, waving away Reese's warning. "You can't expect me *not* to act up in here. Do you see all these people? Who would'a thought they have parties like these in the Meat-Packing District?" She winked at a couple of admirers, grown men clearly old enough to know better. "Girl, there's Miss Fab herself. I gotta go talk to her," Wheez said.

Reese just shook her head. "As long as it's women you're talking to, Wheez. There are too many Chesters in here," she said, speaking of child molesters. "Be careful. And don't embarrass us."

Wheez nodded, then turned serious. "Reese, I've got something to tell you first."

"What is it, Wheez? You being so serious scares me. You don't do serious very well."

Wheez pulled Reese to the side, and then searched the ceiling with her eyes. "Ladies' room sign," she said, pointing. "Let's go." She grabbed Reese's hand, pulling her along until they reached the door. Easily, she pushed it open, and immediately began looking under stall doors. "No feet. It means we're alone."

Reese, for the life of her, couldn't understand why she was mirroring everything Wheez was doing, including looking under stall doors. She caught herself, standing. "What's the big secret that we have to talk about in the toilet?"

Wheez looked at her seriosly. "Broke-Up."

"Hunh?"

Wheez nodded, searching her pocket and purse.

"No apples, Wheez. Talk!"

"Broke-Up. He's not the guy for you, Reese. You need to stay away from him. I can't tell you everything now,

I've been sworn to secrecy. But I'll just say this, lives are at stake."

Now Reese was worried. Was Broke-Up some kind of psycho? Reese nodded at Wheez just to shut her up, but she wasn't really agreeing. Bottom line was she liked Broke-Up, and loved his sound. "If you say so, Wheez. I've always been able to trust you."

Wheez perked. "Cool! Now I feel better about leaving you so I can hang out with the fabulous one. Who knows, maybe she needs me for her show." Wheez slipped away as easily as they'd entered the warehouse. "Toodles, Reese!"

Reese left out of the bathroom, pushing Wheez's information to the back of her mind. She couldn't, wouldn't, stay away from Broke-Up, but she would look for him. Stepping from the restroom, she searched, but still didn't see him. She did spot the bar, and decided it'd be a time killer, plus she was thirsty. Clutching her purse, she made her way over. Her nerves had her shook so bad that they'd absorbed her fluids, and now her mouth was desert dry. It only took seconds for it to be her turn. The bartender eyed her, and she eyed him back. He seemed to be the only one who questioned her age, but she didn't care. The party was full of models who couldn't have been much older than her. Most of them were barely in high school anyway, she assumed as she sized two of them up. "Cranberry juice, low ice," she ordered, then smiled when a look of relief came over the bartender's face.

"What's up? Who you with?" some dude asked, swirling

glass around his drink. A cocktail she could smell a mile away.

Reese sipped her juice, then wiped the cranberry from her ruby-stained lips with the back of her wrist and smiled. She grinned at the guy, realizing that he was studying her hard. Then she had her aha moment. She knew who he was. A heavy-hitting music producer. Just the medicine her career needed, Reese thought, then sipped her drink again. She shrugged. Playing coy with him to get what she wanted was only fair; he seemed to have been trying to peg her since they'd made visual contact. Like she was a celebrity herself, she did what she thought any high-powered, self-assured star would do. She flashed him a smile, turned her back on him, and made her way to the wall of windows. Left the next play to him.

Her arms relaxed and became heavy, hung at her sides, left her just enough strength to grip her drink. The cranberry juice seemed to be toxic as if it had alcohol mixed in it. Her neck warmed and the heat traveled to her head, blurring her mind, making her hope she was wrong. She didn't drink. Drinking was so unsexy. Her lids fell, and her body rocked. Music. Yes, she thought. It had to be the music taking over her. Funky hip-hop that she would've loved to accompany with a piano or violin— any instrument she played—vibrated from the speakers. Then the track switched to a T.I. song, and made her bounce, reminded her that her knees still worked. Her neck was still in commission too, she discovered when some other song mixed in with T.I.'s and caused her head to nod. All alone, Reese began to party in front of the wall of windows. Got into her own groove. It was just she and her natural high. Her juice was just juice, after all.

"Like to do it by yourself, I see," a male voice interrupted her zone.

Reese paused. Stared. Remembered. It was him. The producer. He'd taken the bait after all. "What it wuz, cuz?" she asked him *what's up?* like they did on the rap songs played in the Dirty Dirty. The South. Hotlanta.

The music producer laughed, nodded. "A music person with a sense of humor. I like that."

Reese released her body against the window, and let the glass hold up her weight. "How'd you know I was into music?" she asked, her words blending slowly. Like she was sounding out her question.

He swirled the alcohol in his glass, then held it up like he was toasting. "C'mon. It's an industry party. You're too short and real looking to be a model. You're not sitting over there with the actors. And if you were a rapper or singer, I'd know you. We're always at the same parties. I'm—"

"I know who you are," Reese cut him off, though she didn't remember his handle, just his face. His name wasn't important at the moment. What he could do for her was. "I'm a producer and musician." There, she'd said it. Made the declaration because it was true.

He smiled a different kind of smile. Promising. Cunning. "Let's discuss your *talent* when I get back." He grabbed the glass from her hand before she could down the rest. "You need a refill."

Reese grinned as she watched him move through the crowd to the open bar. Her stare wouldn't have left him if it had not been for a pleasant interruption. A gift who was headed her way. A big-shot record label VP and producer who'd invaded her dreams on countless occasions, one she had hoped to work with one day.

"Aren't you—?"

He nodded, cutting her off, and stopped. He smiled back at her. "Yeah, I'm him. Messiah," was all he said as he began fixing his shirt. Then he bent forward and wiped his kicks.

Reese flushed. His smile was different from Mr. You Need a Refill's. Messiah's held not a trace of slickness, but an energy Reese liked.

"How you?" he asked, unfolding himself and laughing at his feigned Southern accent.

"Great, now that you're here. I'm Reese."

Messiah reared back his head, laughed again like he was responding to a joke. "Oh yeah?" His eyes swept her from head to toe, then traveled up to her perfectly made-up face again. "That's nice, Reese. But you're too young for me. I don't do jailbait."

Reese stood up, leaving the window to mirror her back. She was serious now. "I'm not too young for what I want. I'm here for business."

Messiah crossed his arms. "That should be my cue to walk, but I'm curious. Entertain me. What kind of business you want?" He looked over his shoulder to the bar at the producer Reese had been talking to, then turned, again facing her. "*Him?* You must want him. He does underage. Overage. Any age . . . you get me."

Reese nodded slowly. "Only musically—"

Messiah shook his head, showed he was disgusted. "Not another groupie—"

"No way! I'm nobody's groupie. We were just getting ready to discuss my music."

He put his hand on Reese's shoulder, looked at her intensely. "Say word? You serious? You produce?"

Reese nodded. "Yes, and I play just about every instrument too—and not on a computer. I'm talking live. Keys. Strings. Drums. You name it, and I can play on any kinda track too." She reached into her purse, pulled out an iPod. "Listen to this," she urged, selecting a track and passing him the MP3 player.

He shook his head. Declined.

Reese grabbed his arm. "Please. You gotta! I dressed up, put all this junk on my face so I could look older, and snuck out of the house to be here. Please?"

Messiah smiled, and reluctantly put on the tiny headphones, and began to bop his head to her music. "Got somethin' else on ya? Something for later?"

Reese fished in her bag again, handed him a demo CD, and prayed he wasn't a beat stealer. She'd heard enough about them, but she had to take a chance.

He handed her the iPod. "If you're serious, and I believe you are, I'll listen to this. Pass it around. If you're serious, I mean real serious about your music, I'll be honest with you. You gotta be careful 'cause it's people in this same room who'll act like they're helping you to take advantage of you. So if you're serious about your music, the first thing you have to realize is that these perverts gonna want something from you. The fake ones like ya

boy at the bar." He nodded his head at the super producer. "Be careful if you're dealing with him. Unless, of
course, that's what you wanna do. He'll help you a'right.
Help you get outta yo panties. No such thing as getting
to the top by laying on your back. Not anymore," he
warned.

All Reese could say was, "'Preciate you looking out.
But I'm not laying down to get down. I don't expect anybody to put me on. I can put myself on. I just want a
chance, that's all. I'm dead serious about my music. I've
studied and practiced for years so I can get through the
door."

Messiah nodded. "Good. I'm looking out 'cause you
young and I got a sister, plus you got that thirst. Keep
it—even if you get what you want," he said, then
grabbed her hand. "Matter fact, 'cause you so serious I
got a few *real* industry friends for you to meet. You know
the real ones 'cause we ain't zoned out on drinks and
drugs. We get high off music."

Reese followed Messiah, and was amazed at all the talent in the room. There were musical geniuses who
shamed the predator at the bar she'd spotted slipping
powder into a drink. *Probably my refill.*

Reese sat on the edge of the bed, excitement zooming
through her bones. Her violin was to her left, CDs of
artists she'd seen and met lay to her right. The phone was
pressed to her ear as she watched Wheez sleep, and listened to Broke-Up explain why they wouldn't let him in.
He'd had on the wrong clothes, looked too thugged out,

and he wasn't a girl. Reese didn't care though. She'd made enough connects for them both.

"So you sure you want to do this with me?" he asked.

Reese nodded as if he could see her. "Yes. Can we meet tomorrow? We gotta work now."

"Okay. I'll meet you at your school."

"One more question, Broke-Up?"

"Sure, Reese. What's up?"

She looked over at Wheez to make sure she was still dead to the world. "Is there anything you need to tell me? Are you involved in something dangerous or illegal or wrong?"

Broke-Up laughed. "Yes, I guess. I do deal with killers and go-getters. I make killer beats for the go-getters."

23

ZIGGY

Ziggy stormed through the streets of Harlem, his anger crippling his vision and hearing. All he could focus on was finding a way to pay for school and get his vending cart up and running again. Then he had to get out of his parents' house that he was expected to feel privileged to live in. He was thankful to have a roof over his head, and an occasional good meal filling his belly. But he despised his father's hate and ways. There was no family connection, only his dad's power-fueled hospitality.

"Sandman, you got anything for me yet?" Ziggy asked, walking up to Harlem's unofficial mayor aka Get-It-Anyway-You-Want-It aka Yes-If-The-Price-Is-Right. Sandman could get anybody anything, including a new sky if they had the ends to fund their dream.

Tall and lanky with a shock of white hair, Sandman turned his barely fifty-year-old self around, and grinned. He had absolutely no teeth, and swore he didn't want any. It—toothpaste—was one less hygiene product he had to buy, and, according to him, he didn't miss it. "Ziggy, my man. I know what you need, and got that indeed. Only gonna cost you five-hun'ded."

"Sandman, you know I don't got that type of money! You know I don't. Let's barter."

Sandman zoomed into his own head, obviously in deep thought. He nodded. "Okay. I can barter with you. I will give you a brand-new official vending license in your name, with your picture for . . . five-hun'ded-dollars!" he said, laughing. "What the hell is a barter anyway? I know about the bar, gonna hit that up as soon as you pay me, but I ain't never met a ter. But I'll take that ring."

Ziggy stretched out his hand, looked at his ring, and knew what he had to do. There was no way he'd ever give it to Sandman because he wanted it back. "Cool. I'll be back no later than tomorrow for my license, Sandman. And you better have it!"

There was a pawnshop up the street, Ziggy was sure of that. He'd passed it hundreds, if not thousands, of times before. He hadn't planned on getting rid of his ring on One-two-five, but he had to do what he had to, and it had to be, like, yesterday.

"Z!" someone shouted.

Ziggy turned his head, zipping through the crowded sidewalk, and opened his mouth to speak. "Yuck!" he said, spitting, then he wiped his tongue. A bug had flown in his mouth, and in the process of trying to get rid of it, he'd smashed it on his tongue. Sticking his shirt in his mouth, he searched the street, and saw a bodega two doors down.

The iron-barred door was under his hands before he knew it. Pushing it open with all his power, he darted to the beverage section. He slid the first refrigerated cooler door to the side, grabbed and opened whatever his hand landed on, and washed away any traces of the bug. Better, he walked to the counter, then stopped in his tracks.

Her.

"Hey, Ziggy. We still need to practice our routine . . . if you want to win the competition."

Ziggy smiled. He didn't know she worked in his playground. He remembered to stay cool. "S'up." He set the soda on the counter. "I opened this already. How long you been here?" he asked, wondering how long she'd been working in the neighborhood.

She misunderstood his question. "About four hours. I was just getting ready to leave for the day. I'm supposed to be meeting this dude who's supposed to be partnering with me for this dance audition that's coming up."

Ziggy perked up. "An audition. What kind?"

"Commercial stuff. Videos. Nothing you'd be interested in, Mr. Professional Choreographer. They give you moves to follow, then, if picked, you get to showcase your own." She shrugged. "I don't know, that part might work for you."

Ziggy nearly lost his cool. Never mind what he wouldn't do before. Now he had to do all he could. He needed cash as badly as he needed breath. "But I *am* interested. Very. Can't you just shake that dude, and partner with me instead? We—me and you—already got a flow."

"You sure, Ziggy? It doesn't pay much. We'll only get

like five bills for a lot of videos. It's more exposure work."

He almost lost it. Almost. She'd just stood in front of him, dangled the five-hundred-dollar bait he needed, and he was going to bite. They'd be chosen, he'd see to that. "I got us. Let's go to the school and practice now. You are getting off, right?"

The walk was short, but a long one. Ziggy couldn't wait to kick off his shoes and feel the hardwood under his feet. All the way there he'd imagined steps for them. Ones for him, others for her, and a routine or two they could swing together if given the opportunity.

"Your head's nodding. What music are you hearing?" she asked.

"Hip-hop. I think we need straight hardcore rap to groove to. We can freak it with a bit of reggae, then twist them with a samba-infused number. Blow their minds, ya know?"

She nodded, walking through the door as Ziggy held it open.

"Keep quiet," he said. "You know staff may still be buzzing around, and we're not supposed to be here after hours. Let's go to the music studio and see what type of hip-hop we can borrow, then we'll go to the dance room at the end of the hall."

The hallway was almost eerie when it was empty. Ziggy had never really been alone in the school. He was used to it bustling with some sort of happenings going on. There was always someone singing, rapping, dancing, and acting.

Her hand was on his arm, stopping him. "You hear that? Sound like someone fell."

Ziggy listened, but all he could hear was the beat of his own heart. He shrugged. They'd just have to take a chance because they needed the studio, and she hadn't offered for them to practice in her basement, so he assumed it was off limits. They were in front of the music room in seconds. Ziggy put his finger to his lip to signal that she should still be quiet. Carefully he pushed open the door.

"Ziggy!" Half-Dead shouted. "What up, dancer of the year?"

Ziggy's eyes widened. What the heck was Half-Dead doing in the school after hours? He was just about to speak when something else caught his attention.

Broke-Up.

"Who a dancer?" Broke-Up asked.

Half-Dead looked back and forth between the brothers. "I knew you looked familiar, Broke-Up. I told you that you look like some dude here who dances. This is him. Ziggy."

In less than a second, Broke-Up and Ziggy were on the floor, locking horns as if they were bulls. They'd never had a real fist fight in their life, but no one would've been able to tell.

"Batty boy, you!"

"Break it up. Break it up!" Mrs. Allen said, running into the room, trying to separate Ziggy and his brother. "What's the meaning of this?" She craned her neck, then cocked it to the side. "What's that I hear? Hip-hop? In my school? Reese?! Not today, not after I just left a late meeting where I heard the school may be closing." She clasped her hand over her mouth, obviously realizing her mistake.

"That's me and Reese's music. . . ." Broke-Up began proudly, still trying to fight Ziggy, then quieted when he realized the seriousness of what Mrs. Allen said.

24

JAMAICA-KINCAID

No. *Nope. Absolutely not.* All Jamaica needed was another dictator on the scene to tell her how bad she was, then clean it up with how good she could be. Talia was like Maritzio—a walking, talking, oxymoron who was indecisive when it came to her, apparently. Either she was good at acting or she wasn't. At the moment, she didn't care. All she could focus on was getting her lines right, then shuttling off to the train station so she could meet her parents at their hotel. And Talia, for the last few rehearsals, had made acting hellish for her. She didn't know if it was because Maritzio was out of the country and couldn't change his schedule, or if the lady was just hard to work for. What she really couldn't understand was why all the investment in her. If she wasn't as good as Talia wanted her to be, and believed she could help her become, why go to the trouble? Talia could've always cast another actress, one "seasoned" enough. Jamaica shrugged. She wouldn't ask; that'd be too much like killing her own dream. She'd roll with it. Spin with it until it moved with ease.

"Yes. Yes. Yes," Talia kept saying over and over, urging Jamaica. "Aha. Aha. Aha."

She turned, walked, said her lines until she felt she was talking in circles, did and said the exact same thing over and over as her warm-up. This was the part of the acting instruction that tickled her. Why Talia thought her idea was best was beyond Jamaica, but she did it anyway. Whatever it took to keep her part until Maritzio arrived, she'd do. Sure, it wasn't her way. It was still a means, that's what she kept telling herself. Memorizing lines, going off script to add in real-life flavor, turning on and off emotion were the easiest things to her, like breathing. Until she saw Maritzio walking in. That's when she froze.

"Where's this gift you mentioned?" Maritzio boomed with a slight smile on his face. A tinge of excitement lit his eyes, if, in fact, he could feel any.

Talia walked up to where he stood, pointed at Jamaica, then beckoned her over.

"*Her?*" he said, pointing. "Talia, you've got to be kidding, yes?" Maritzio laughed. "No. No. *No*. I won't work with her. Again."

Jamaica couldn't help smiling. What was up with these two? Did they always triple talk? Talia had her "Yes. Yes. Yes." and "Aha Aha Aha" and Maritzio had his "No. No. No."

It took everything she had in her, every ounce of control she had, not to sneer at, hit, or throw a shoe at him. She'd had enough of him, of Talia too, but there was something brewing, and she would wait it out, not kill it by verbalizing her jazzy thoughts.

"Look! Just look, Maritzio. You too, Jamaica," Talia ordered them, surfing through electronic clips of an earlier rehearsal. "Tell me she isn't *it*?" she dared Maritzio. "See what I mean, Jamaica? Either I will dislike you or love you. *Make* me love you. Look at how fantastic your scenes are."

Maritzio ran his hands through his hair, then rubbed his beard. He looked from Jamaica to the small screen, then back at Jamaica again. "You relaxed," he told—not asked—her, then peeled his blazer off, and snatched up a clipboard. "Stay relaxed for me. No intimidation, Jamaica. I want exactly what you gave the last director when you rehearsed, then more. Go! Go! Go!" he ordered in triplicate, rushing her to begin.

Jamaica moved right into character. Paused and tried to find her rhythm, but couldn't. She tried again and failed again.

"Stop!" Maritzio walked up to her. "What's the problem? Me?"

Jamaica shook her head. "Not you."

"Think for a moment. What made you act like you did earlier? You were more comfortable, it showed."

"Breathe," Talia interrupted. "Jamaica exhaled before her scenes. I heard her. We all did. Her breathing was like music. Yes, it was like she had her own music."

Jamaica crinkled her nose. Was her breathing that apparent? She shrugged, and guessed so. Then she smiled. "I did. Breathing is like a song playing in my head. Let's start again," she told Maritzio, glad that she could give them what they wanted so she could hurry and leave to get to her parents.

"Wonderful! Absolutely wonderful!" Maritzio praised when she'd run through her lines, and they were finally finished. "Wish we could've connected before like this, Jamaica. You"—he pinched her cheek as if she were his child—"are going to make us and you a lot of money. You are *it*."

"Get ready. Your life is going to change." Talia smiled.

Jamaica scooped up her book bag, waved, and ran out the door so her life could do just that, change before her parents discovered her secret and snatched it. But, it may've been too late, she feared when she read her sister's text message, and almost cried from the one Mateo sent seconds after.

EVIL SISTER: THE BEAUTY QUEEN AND GURU R ON 2 U

MATEO: SKOOL MIGHT CLOSE BCUZ NO $$$

25

LA-LA

La-La tried to swallow her embarrassment, but couldn't. Ziggy stood in the doorway—in her project building—and she was sure he'd expire from the scent of alcohol and urine that assaulted her nose from where she stood, that someone, probably the knuckleheaded teenage gangbangers, had christened the hallway with. Ziggy had to smell it too, she guessed from the way he poked out his lips as if he were trying to block his nostrils. A slight smile spread on her face. With his upper lip flipped up a bit, he resembled a cute fish.

Her eyebrows rose as she admired him. She thought about asking him what he was doing there and how he'd found out where she lived, but she didn't want to be rude.

"Hi," she said instead.

He waved as if he were down the hall instead of only inches away. "Aren't you going to let me in? Or . . . you can't? Some girls' mothers don't play—"

Something sharp poked La-La in the back and made her grit her teeth. She cleared her throat, cutting off Ziggy. "Let him in, La-La," Remi whispered from behind, jabbing her again with an ink pen. "Boom-Kesha's not here to embarrass you."

Ziggy tilted his head, then leaned to the side, trying to zoom in on Remi. "Hello, whoever you are," he said to her, waving and smiling.

Remi giggled.

La-La stepped to the side. "Sorry for being rude, but the place is a mess—"

"Because we're cleaning up. And, you know, sometimes you have to mess up to clean up," Remi cut in, lying. She walked in front of Ziggy, and extended her hand like a businesswoman. Her headscarf accidentally slipped from her forehead, revealing a fraction of her hairless scalp. Immediately, she fixed it with a look of panic on her face. It was clear that she was embarrassed—horrified—but she smiled. "I'm Remi."

La-La watched in half-horror as Ziggy's eyes stretched slightly in surprise, then went back to normal. He matched Remi's smile, and it was genuine. "I'm Ziggy." He turned to La-La. "Are you ready for the pool party? That's why I'm here . . . and to tell you about the school."

"Cyd and Rikki told me about the school. There's gotta be something we can do. One sec, okay? I'll be back," she said, rushing off to her room where she stripped out of her clothes, and slipped into the panties and bra that were going to serve as her swimming suit. She twirled in the mirror, stopping only to look at her butt. Rikki had been right, she did look curvier. She layered an outfit Cyd had picked out for her to wear over the faux swim gear, grabbed a small book bag, and headed to the door. A smile parted her lips before she made it down the hall. Ziggy was gaining more and more of her heart every time she saw him. Like now. He and Remi were conversing like old friends, slapping five, and giving each other a pound. He didn't seem to be the least bit affected by her sister's illness like so many others—including Boom-Kesha, their mother.

"I'm ready," she made herself interrupt, but not because she wanted to. It was time to go, and she wanted to spend every available minute she could with Ziggy.

Ziggy gave Remi another pound, put his hat on her head, then pulled her into a slight hug. "A'ight, lil sis. Next week, that's my word. Promise."

Before they'd made it out of the building, Ziggy stopped in his tracks. "You know your sister's a good kid. I like her. It's too bad about her dis-ease." He pronounced disease as two separate words, making it sound better. "Because that's what she has . . . some uneasiness. There's no way you can make me believe that the spunky girl I just met is sick—"

"Oh *no?*" a voice cut in that made La-La roll her eyes. Boom-Kesha. "Well, Remi *is* sick, and who are you? Bringing your fresh behind over here? Who're you smelling under? La-La?"

"What up, Pop-po?" Paco asked, coming out of nowhere with a bottle of beer in a paper bag in one hand. He gave Ziggy a pound like they knew one another.

"My mother and her boyfriend. Drunks," La-La whispered to Ziggy. "Sorry."

Ziggy greeted the adults, ignoring Boom-Kesha's remarks.

"You heard me? I *said* she's sick," Boom-Kesha repeated, then uttered to Paco: "Like he can't see she's *bald*. He must think we're fools or something." She turned to La-La, then touched her hair. "This is the one with all the beautiful good hair."

La-La moved away from her mother, and wanted to cry. Remi stood behind her with tears in her eyes.

La-La zoomed down the street. She didn't want to look at Ziggy. Didn't want him to see the hurt in her eyes or face the truth that her decision would possibly push him away.

"Where we going?" Ziggy asked, running behind her. "La-La, wait up!" He ran up to her, and grabbed her hand.

She stopped, and took a long stare at him. "Ziggy, do you like me only because of my hair?"

Ziggy laughed. "No. It's a bonus, but that's not what I like about you, not the only thing. I like your style, drive. Why?"

"There's somewhere I want to go, something I need to do. And I want you to go with me."

"But the party . . ."

La-La shook her head. "Can we skip it?"

Ziggy shrugged. "Sure, there's another one soon. And it's a hotel indoor pool party where you can sing, and we can raise money to save the school. But you may not want to be at that one. Nakeeda's going to be there."

La-La snaked her neck. "Eff Nakeeda."

She looked at Ziggy for a sign, any inclination as to whether she should be concerned or not. His eyes didn't *say* anything, but they did ask if she was sure or not. She nodded her head.

"Don't move. Okay?" the barber said, moving the clippers along the side of her head.

Her hair, her once beautiful and thick locks, lay in her lap with rubber bands on one end of each pigtail that'd been clipped off before the actual barbering begun. She was tired of her sister suffering alone, and though cutting off her hair wouldn't make Remi's grow back faster, La-La believed she could lift her spirits. At least they'd go through the growing process together.

Ziggy raised his brows when she was finished, walking around the chair inspecting La-La's Caesar cut. "It looks good. Really good. I wasn't sure you could pull this off, but it sorta adds to you."

La-La smiled. "You think? I'm not too skinny for this, right? I don't want to look like a corpse from an old MJ video. My teeth are bad enough. I need braces. I don't want to look like a raggedy-mouth crackhead," she said, then covered her mouth. She didn't want him to see her teeth. Now she'd gone and drawn attention to them.

Ziggy laughed, then patted her leg. "Nothing's wrong with your teeth. Don't get caught up in the American hype. Orthodontics is an American thing. Now get up. My turn. For Remi, I'm going bald."

She knew she liked him for a reason.

26

REESE

ME: MEETING MESSIAH @ STUDIO. TOLD ME TO BRING STRINGS.

BROKE-UP: CAN'T MAKE IT. TAKE BEATS & KILL 'EM. U GOT THIS.

With a violin tucked under her arm, Reese stood with a crowd in front of the subway doors waiting for the train to stop. She looked at her watch. 6:45. Messiah had told her he was leaving around six o'clock, give or take a few. Closing her eyes, she prayed he was still there, that he wasn't angry or thinking she wasn't serious. She would've called the studio, but didn't know the name of it. All she had were the cross streets.

The doors opened with a ding, interrupting her worry. She pushed past the couple of riders who were exiting too slowly. She rounded the doorway, then hauled her behind down the platform and up the stairs. Out of breath, she bent forward a little, collected herself while rereading the cross streets.

"Right," she directed her feet to pound the pavement. The studio was to the right, up four blocks, then over two more to the left. "Excuse me. Excuse me." Reese zipped through the crowded Manhattan sidewalk, accidentally bumping a pedestrian or two. "Sorry," she yelled behind her, sure she'd made someone connect with the ground. Her violin case bumped her leg as she made haste, turning the corner, closer than ever to her destination.

There it was. Reese stopped, looked up, saw it was on the second floor. She was tired from the long seven-block run, but not too worn out to go after her dream. Collecting her cool, she straightened up, entered the building. Her eyes searched for the stair doors after she'd pressed the elevator button, and waited two seconds too long. The climb, tackled by exhausted legs, was tedious.

"Can I help you?" a receptionist asked.

"I'm supposed to be meeting Messiah here," Reese said, smiling.

The receptionist returned the smile. "One sec." She picked up the phone, dialed, and spoke to someone. "I'm sorry, but he's gone. I thought he'd just walked out, but I wanted to be sure."

"Just as in *just*, just? Like seconds or minutes ago?"

"Seconds."

Reese slapped the counter. "Thanks!"

"Try the bodega on the corner. He goes there a lot for the heros," the lady shouted from behind.

Reese grimaced as her feet pounded against the cement staircase as she descended the stairs. She shot through the door, paused outside in front of the building, looked to her right, then her left in search of the bodega. There it was, sitting on the corner.

"Excuse me!" Reese repeated her same apologies as she made her way through the crowd until she reached the bodega. She snatched open the door, scanning the store with her eyes. There was no Messiah in sight. She felt like melting into one big tear and puddling the floor. But then someone caught her attention. A man walking out the bodega's other door she hadn't known existed, but she couldn't see his face. It had to be him though. "You, there! Messiah? Wait up. Is that you Messiah?" she ran toward the other door.

He turned with a smile and, as the receptionist told her, a hero. He held up the bag the sandwich was housed in. "Fuel. Did you eat yet?"

Reese shook her head. *Eat?* She'd been too excited to do anything after he'd called and told her he needed live strings for a huge R & B star. That's what he'd said, but he never mentioned a name. "I'm okay. It's not good to play on a full stomach. It gets me tired."

"Cool," he said. "Follow me. And whatever you do, Reese, act professional. I'm not implying you won't, I'm just asking you not to become a groupie. These artists are no different than us. And this one's huge. Her name alone will garner you more work."

Reese nodded, taking mental notes. She wondered who was waiting in the studio, who would be grooving to her strings. It didn't take long for her to be able to answer the questions plaguing her mind. As soon as they entered the sound room, Reese almost passed out from excitement. Before her stood the woman she'd listened to for years, the woman who sat next to the man the rap industry hailed as king.

"Hello," the beautiful lady with the blond lace-front weave said. "I hear you're going to play the strings?"

And Reese did play her strings. She worked her violin until the strings popped, but she didn't care. She'd come with plenty, and had used just as many by the time the session ended.

The pretty lady who'd sung for the president, had her own clothing line, was on commercials, and was recognized by her first initial walked over to Reese, nodding and smiling. "I like your drive. Do you have anything else? My album's not finished."

Reese, not wanting to step on Messiah's toes, looked over to him for approval.

He gave her a hard head nod and thumbs-up.

Smiling, Reese reached into her book bag, took out a CD of the music she and Broke-Up made, and handed it over. "Here's just a sample, and, of course, I can do live accompaniment."

27

ZIGGY

Broke-Up told their father. Ziggy's life was over, he was homeless, and without family. He was sure. As much as he'd loved his brother, today was different. He felt like he'd been employing the enemy and helping his dreams, while he was a killer of Ziggy's. He walked down the street, blending into the Harlem night. He'd been holing himself up at Rikki's, but he couldn't stay there anymore. They could only hide him for so long before her mother caught on. Sticking his hands in his pockets, Ziggy kicked an empty beer bottle, and watched as it skipped across the concrete and, finally, landed in the gutter. He knew exactly what that bottle felt like. Used. Unappreciated. Discarded.

Whatever.

The wind blew a slight breeze past his shoulders, and made him shiver. He pushed his hands deeper into his pockets as if searching for the answer in his jeans. What he needed to do was easy to figure out. It was the how that was killing him. How was he supposed to pay for school, an apartment or room, and a vending license? He was only a freshman, too young to get a full-time on-the-books job. He looked at his watch. The only chance he had to secure himself and money situation was the upcoming video audition. He had managed to practice with whatever-her-name-is a couple of times, and he was sure one of them would be picked, if not both.

The concrete sounded hollow under his feet as he climbed the stoop. He was prepared for the worst, had even played the possible argument between him and his father in his head. Still though, he wasn't looking forward to it. Reaching for the door, he jumped back. Broke-Up had beat him to it, pushing open the screen door.

"Walk with me, Star," Broke-Up said, walking out of the brownstone.

Ziggy scowled at his brother. "Say word. Now you want to talk. You was all fists and gay this, gay that before. Why you want to talk to me now? I'm twinkle toes, remember?"

Broke-Up patted Ziggy on the back, sucking his teeth.

Ziggy flinched, ready to fight.

"Stoppit, Z. I don't want to fight you."

Ziggy pushed up on his brother, bucking his chest against Broke-Up's. "Yeah? So what if I do? You do know you disrespected me, shamed the family . . ." Ziggy spit. "I'm sorry, I'm the one who shamed the family. Right? That's the sentence?"

Broke-Up grabbed Ziggy by his shoulders, and pushed

him back arm's length. Both of them almost fell on the steps. "Yo, Star. Shuddup. You want Pops to hear you? He already beefing about you not coming home for days, you want him to know you dance too?"

A new energy floated through Ziggy. "*Word?*" Broke-Up hadn't told. He couldn't believe it. He was sure that would've been the first thing he'd do. Snitch.

They posted up by the telephone pole on the corner. Ziggy leaned against it, digging his hands in his pockets. Broke-Up stood banging his fist in his palm with each point he made. From a distance one wouldn't be able to tell one brother from the other, they resembled each other that much. But their outer appearance wasn't the only common trait they shared.

"So, what'chu think?" Broke-Up said, hanging his head.

Ziggy just looked at his brother. He couldn't be sure he'd heard what his ears were trying to convince him he had.

"Did you hear me, Z? So can you hook me up? I want to produce more than anything, and I believe I can make it happen on my own. But if you get me in your school, I *know* I can make it happen," he said, crossing his arms. "And it'll help me start these classes I've been thinking about. I want to help these little knuckleheads around here. Maybe if they learn something they won't be headed to jail before they hit high school."

Ziggy dug his index fingers in both his ears and shook them. Either something was lodged in his canals or he was hallucinating. Broke-Up wanted to go to his school and help children? "Wow."

"Z!"

Snapping back to reality, he nodded. "So if I get you in, you won't tell and you're going to help kids?"

Broke-Up nodded. "And if you don't pawn your ring."

His hands were on her waist, lifting her and flinging her like he was throwing her across the room. With a long reach, Ziggy snatched her back, folded her in a backwards U, then stepped over her, picking her up until her feet came just over his shoulders. Her hands were wrapped on his ankles while he C walked across the dance floor. He looked in the floor-to-ceiling mirrors, almost shook his head at them. They were freaking it. They looked like they were. He felt like they were. With one look over at the judges with raised eyebrows, and awe on their faces, he knew, without a doubt, they definitely were.

The track ended just as Ziggy flipped her around like a watch's second hand, and brought her face to his. Their synchronization was incredible, and timing perfect.

"Thank you," she whispered to him as the judges signaled their turn was up.

"Don't thank me until we win."

She looked over at the judges, pointed her finger. "I don't know how good your vision is, but I can spot that big red *yes* they wrote by our names. So, as I said, thank you. Make sure you spend your loot wisely."

28

JAMAICA-KINCAID

Jamaica leaned against the dirty bathroom wall, looking at her watch. Time was running out, and she couldn't have been more pleased. She'd been cooped up in the ladies' restroom for more than an hour, waiting to make her exit. Her wheeled suitcase was next to her with a laptop bag on top, and she had a book bag on her back with her old school name embroidered on it. She looked at herself in the dirty mirror, walked over to the sink, and turned on the faucet. Sticking her hands under the cold stream, she wet her hands, then patted her face. Today was going to be the best acting role in her life. It had to be for her to stay in New York. Her parents would be there to pick her up any minute, and she had to look like she'd just gotten off the train. One more look at her wrist, and she exhaled. It was showtime.

Pushing through the throng of people, she pulled her luggage behind her, then painted on an I'm-tired-from-the-train-but-I'm-happy-to-see-you look. She moved through the crowd and lines of people waiting for the doors to open so they could board their respective trains, then turned right. Headed toward the thirty-fourth Street exit, but she didn't make it.

"Jamaica-Kincaid, dah-ling," her mother's voice was clean and crisp, cutting through the muttering of the crowd.

Jamaica turned, waving. Picking up speed, she fell into a slight run, wheeling her bag behind her. "Mother! Father!"

It was a Hallmark moment. Her mother ran, meeting her halfway, and wrapped her in her arms. She planted thousands of little kisses all over Jamaica's face, then handed her off to her dad. He picked her up, and spun her around. They were a sight seldom before seen, and the train station patrons watched them as if they were aliens at a skate rink.

"Is this all you have?" Mother asked, looking at Jamaica's suitcase as if it had the flu and was contagious. "I'll replace that ASAP."

Her father waved away her mother's excuse for shopping. "Come, sweetheart, let's go eat and get reacquainted.

Jamaica laughed. How she was supposed to get reacquainted with the two who knew her better than any other people in the world, she could never figure out, but he always said it. To make him happy, she never questioned him. He was, after all, her father: her protector and bank account.

The limo was as severe as she'd imagined. It was a

stretch on steroids, and Jamaica wondered if her parents had ever been in a regular car. Did they even drive? She'd never seen either of them behind the wheel, and she found it a bit disturbing. The whole I'm-super-rich thing made her uncomfortable, and she didn't know why. They'd never really acted better than anyone. Okay, just once or twice. But they were nice people, a little extra, but happy and welcoming.

"I thought we'd do lunch, then head over to some-where special. We have a surprise for you I'm sure you'll enjoy."

She perked up now. "Really? What kind?"

Her mother reached over and patted her leg. The per-fect smile spread across her perfectly made-up face, re-vealing her perfect veneers. "Dah-ling it wouldn't be a surprise if we told you."

Jamaica nodded, and felt "acting" taking its toll on her. Her lids were heavy, and she needed a power nap. If only for ten minutes. "Can you wake me when we get there? I'm a bit tired from the train. You know I can never rest around that many people," she fattened her lie.

Father smiled, then nodded. "Sure. Get your rest. With this traffic, we've plenty of time."

The ride, though taken in a plush limo, was a bumpy one, and each rock of the car lulled Jamaica into a deeper sleep. Faintly, she could overhear her parents whisper loudly. Horns blew, the limo jerked to a stop, then took off again after a couple of minutes. *Traffic light,* thought Jamaica. Smells of different types of foods made their way into the car, turning her stomach. She was hungrier than she'd thought, and was just about to open her eyes and ask when they'd arrive at the restaurant, but her mother stopped her.

"Brad, honey? Are you sure she told you Jamaica's acting and living here?"

Oh-no-oh-no-oh-no. So her sister was right—her parents were on to her, and pretending they didn't know a thing. Obviously, she wasn't the only actor in the limo. Smarter than they'd probably given her credit for, Jamaica kept her eyes closed until she felt the limo come to another complete stop. Her adrenaline raced, and her eyes shot open. Quickly, she grabbed her book bag from next to her, then jumped out of the car.

"Jamaica-Kincaid, where are you going?" her mother's voice called to her back.

"Jamaica!" her father's voice said, then faded as she snaked her way through the crowded sidewalk, headed toward whatever train or taxi she could get to first. There was no way she was going to let them take her back to Connecticut. She hadn't come this far, worked this hard, grown up so much that she was going to hand it all over without a fight. But they'd have to find and catch her first.

29

LA-LA

The ritzy hotel's pool area was lively and welcoming, quite the opposite of how she'd imagined the backyard cookout pool party that she'd missed due to her haircut. La-La smiled. The slight breeze from the ventilation system blew on the back of her neck, giving her goose bumps. She looked to her right, then thought better. Ziggy was the one who gave her the chills. It was nice to walk in with him by her side, and even better to be his official date. It seemed all eyes were on them, and it didn't bother her one iota. She was impressed that he'd even taken her at all. After all, he was the guy to be with, the one plenty of girls wanted. But he was with her, she kept reminding herself. They'd kissed, gotten their hair shaved together, and he'd shown up at all of her performances. He was, without a doubt, her boyfriend.

His hand was on her back, ushering her toward a lounger. "You want something to drink?"

La-La nodded, then began disrobing. Her shoes were first, then her jeans. She noticed he'd offered to go get drinks, but was still standing next to her. His eyes watched her carefully, and weren't apologetic. Suddenly, she was nervous. Yes, she had her "bathing suit" on, but, still, she felt awkward. It didn't matter how much padding or lift the bra serving as a bikini top added, she was light in the chest, and she didn't want him to see. "You're just going to stand there?"

Ziggy smiled and nodded. "I'm going to see anyway. You act like you're naked underneath." He laughed. "Okay. Okay. I'll go get you a soda."

When his back was turned, she freed herself of the shirt, then heard laughter. She looked in the direction he was supposed to be walking in, and tsked. He'd stopped feet from her, but his eyes were on her.

"Nice," he complimented.

La-La waved him away, then sat on the lounger. Before she could stretch her feet in front of her, the devil and her crony made an appearance. Nakeeda and Hammerhead-Helen. Nakeeda swung a black plastic bag back and forth, eyeing La-La.

"So . . . you're here with Z." It wasn't a question.

La-La just looked at her. No, there was no such thing as a stupid question, but there was certainly such thing as an unnecessary statement. But she shouldn't have been surprised. Almost everything about Nakeeda was un-called for. Like that chipped tooth she refused to get fixed, and her inflamed gums that snitched on her bad hygiene. Her poor choice of going braless in the yellow sundress was also bad. As was her choice of a hangout partner.

"Yeah," Hammerhead-Helen added with authority, like she was saying something no one had before heard.

La-La just looked at both of them. She hadn't the time or the energy, and she didn't have the nerve to stand up for herself like she wished she did. She didn't know what it was about Nakeeda that made her bones freeze, but she didn't have the boldness Cyd would've had. "Please, just go away."

Nakeeda did the unthinkable. She laced her arm through Hammerhead-Helen's, and did just that. Walked away, swinging the black plastic bag.

La-La closed her eyes, and relaxed a little. Remi had her last dose of chemo coming up, and she felt better. Radiation was supposed to be worse, according to the few people in the hospital who would talk around a teenager, but she had all the confidence in the world that her sister would get better. They were halfway home.

"Ooh, shuckey duckey now!" Rikki's voice made her open her eyes.

"Alrighty, Ms. Mighty," Cyd added.

La-La sat up, glad to see her two friends. She'd called them earlier to make sure they were coming, and they hadn't let her down.

Cyd pointed behind. "Did you see the devil and the big-headed girl? Yeesh, that girl's head is huge. I'm talking should-be-studied-by-science large."

La-La nodded. "Unfortunately."

Rikki sat next to La-La, making room for herself on the one-person lounger. "So you gonna sing today, hunh?"

"Yes, of course I am. Ziggy's come up with a plan so we can raise money for the school. And a little more exposure never hurt." She reached into her tote, then handed them each a flyer Ziggy had had printed. Her picture was on the front of it, along with SAVE HARLEM ACADEMY OF THE CREATIVE AND PERFORMING ARTS.

"This is dope," Rikki said. "Right, Cyd?"

Cyd didn't answer. Her head was turned, and her jaw was to the floor.

"Cyd?" said Rikki.

No answer. Cyd just pointed her finger.

Rikki craned her neck in the direction Cyd's index was pointed, then closed her eyes, and covered her face with her hands.

La-La stood. She knew her best friend, and it took a whole heck of a lot to make Cyd quiet. She got up and walked over next to Cyd, then moved her eyes in the direction Cyd pointed. "Un-unh."

Her feet carried her in a hurry toward the juice bar, but she couldn't get her there fast enough. The wet tile stuck to her feet, then released making a sucking noise. She told herself that she was seeing things, that her vision was blurry and deceiving, but she knew it was a lie. Ziggy stood there, clear as day, holding the black plastic bag Nakeeda had been swinging. Nakeeda was pressed against him, her mouth on his. They were kissing.

In less than three steps, La-La knew she'd reach them. She didn't know what she'd do when they were face-to-face, but they'd all find out. Suddenly, Ziggy was pulling away from Nakeeda, then almost pushing her down.

"What the—? Nakeeda, what you do that for? *Ill!* I didn't ask you to buy me dance shoes." He wiped his mouth with the back of his wrist, turned his head, and locked eyes with La-La.

Then her name came over the speakers. Despite a broken heart, disappointment, embarrassment, and wanting to take a stand, the show had to go on. She had to sing. And she vowed to blow the heck out of the song as a way to tell both Ziggy and Nakeeda they could kiss her flat behind since her mouth couldn't form the words.

30

REESE

She was convinced her mother was selfish and insane, and she was adopted. There was no way that her mom had ever truly been in love with music, or she would've appreciated different kinds of it. If she had, she must've lost her passion, and was now scorned because she hadn't made it. Jilted. *Those who don't do, teach.* Someone must've crushed her mother's dreams badly, and she must've vowed to take her grief out on her daughter. Yes, Mrs. Allen would make sure that she had company in the land of the miserable. Because of her mother's heartlessness, Reese would die of shame and want. Her mom had already embarrassed her in front of Broke-Up, and showed no signs of budging or compromising.

That lady, Mrs. Allen, director of Harlem Academy, the one who kept insisting that she birthed Reese and pretended to be her mother, wouldn't leave her alone. She was banging on her door, trying to kill her dream, and her knocking was as persistent as a gravedigger digging a plot. As much as she'd tried to convince her, Reese knew she wasn't her mother. She couldn't possibly have been. If she were, she'd have understood her, or at least tried to. She would've accepted that Reese could prepare for Julliard and produce at the same time.

"Here," her mother yelled, jiggling her doorknob, unable to turn it. "Ree-eese Al-len! Un . . . lock . . . this . . . door . . . now!" She was demanding, spitting out each syllable of Reese's name as if it were a complex word. They'd gone through it the whole afternoon—the past week or more, really—and not once had she been able to get Reese to open her door after she'd locked it. One would think that her mother would have caught on, but she didn't. And adults had the nerve to think teens were stupid?

ME: NOT GOING 2 OPEN DOOR & SHE KNOWS IT

BROKE-UP: TALK 2 HER. CONVINCE HER

ME: CAN'T. THAT'S WHY I'M IN HERE. TAKING A STAND. NEVER CHALLENGED HER B4

Mrs. Allen yelled through the door: "Fine. Have it your way, and I'll have mine." She slid a yellowed piece of paper under Reese's door.

Her birth certificate.

Reese got up, and picked it up. She looked at it, and felt sick.

Yuck. Mrs. Allen was, without a doubt, her mother. Reese groaned loud enough for her mother to hear, knowing that it'd ruffle her feathers more. As a director and teacher, Mrs. Allen always hated verbal sounds that weren't words.

"I told you I'm your mother and, right now, I almost regret it as much as you do. Now unlock this door."

"Can't. It's stuck," Reese lied.

"And you'll be stuck when your father comes home, and I tell him you've been producing!"

"I'm home now," her father's voice sounded off from the other side. "I told you I was getting in three hours ago, and I was waiting for you to pick me up. And she'll be stuck why?"

Reese jumped up and unlocked the door. She had to. Her father's voice was different. Angry. And as much as she didn't want to depend on him, she knew he was an option. He was in the music business so he had to understand.

"What's going on, Reese?" he asked, leaning against the wall. He looked tired.

Mrs. Allen cut in. "She's been sneaking and producing that . . . that . . . garbage."

She couldn't believe her eyes, but her father actually looked impressed. He raised his brows. "Really? You know, I started out producing. I was never any good, but I tried while I was interning."

"'Really?' That's *all* you have to say?" Her mother was fuming. "Do you know how much I've invested in her, and now she wants to throw it away. I've made contacts at Julliard, schmoozed with people on the board. I've done everything."

"But listen to my music. All I asked is for you to listen, to give me a chance to produce and study so I can try to get in Julliard one day—for you. I don't want Julliard, Mom. You do."

Reese didn't know if He was trying to wage war or not, but He looked at them both, then set down his bag, and walked toward Reese. "Mind letting me take a listen? I'd like to hear."

She smiled, glad that He wanted to listen to her music. She wondered how far she could take it. "If you like, there's a contest going on tonight. Me and my partner are supposed to compete. It's sorta like a DJ contest, but it's for young producers."

He nodded, then transformed back into her dad. "Yes, that'll be great." He nodded. "Just great. If I don't know anything else, I know music. Remember, the job you always get upset with me for?"

She'd never really considered that. He was also in love with music. Maybe they had more in common than she'd believed.

31

ZIGGY

Sandman sang "Gonna Have a Funky Good Time," at the top of his lungs. Snapping his fingers, he danced on the corner. He shuffled his feet back and forth, did the older version of the two-step. He cupped his hands around his mouth. "And get high . . . er!"

Ziggy watched him as he approached, nodding his head to the old James Brown tune Sandman was singing. He'd come carrying the five hundred dollars for the vending license, and he couldn't be happier. He felt like embarrassing himself, and getting down on the corner with the older dude. "Sandman! What it do?"

Sandman turned, still singing. He waved his hand, then started doing the wop, electric slide, and whatever else he could fit in during the short tune that he'd extended and remixed with his words. "Z! What you got, baby boy? What'chu know about this here? Hunh, youngin'?"

Ziggy dug in his pocket, and pulled out five hundred-dollar bills. "I got this, Sandman. Your money."

Sandman switched tunes, singing something that sounded like a cross between Al Green and Teddy Pendergrass. He popped his fly-guy seventies collar, then straightened the sleeves on his suit. "That's what I'm talkin' 'bout, young-in'. It don't mean a thing if it ain't got that money ring. Brrrinnng," he made the sound of a telephone ring, laughing and showing his gums. He took the money, held it in his palm, and closed his eyes. Chanting, then mumbling, he opened his lids. "Had to pray over it, make sure it ain't bad." He slapped his thigh, then broke out in laughter. Finally, he reached inside his suit coat, pulled out a huge eight by eleven envelope, and dug through it until he came across Ziggy's stuff.

Ziggy looked at him cross-eyed, wondering where he'd kept that large mustard envelope. They didn't make jacket pockets that big. He shrugged. Knowing Sandman, he'd made it happen. You couldn't put anything past him.

"Thanks. So we good?" he asked, taking his documents.

Sandman nodded, turned his back as if he hadn't just had an exchange with Ziggy, then began singing and dancing again. "Good with what, youngin'? I don't know what'chu talking about."

His palms were sweating, and anxiousness flowed through his veins. Ziggy shifted back and forth, from side to side. It was good energy, that's what he told himself. He always had this pep talk with himself before a competition. On the surface, he was all calm and smooth. Inside, he had butterflies like a teenage girl in love. But it was cool. "Whatever works."

"You ready, Z?" asked Rikki, standing beside him in a ZIGGY FOR PRESIDENT shirt that she'd obviously made herself. The crooked letters, slanted upward, were a dead giveaway. But it was the thought that counted.

He just looked at her.

"Right. Right. No talking until after the comp. I remember." She pointed. "Here comes La-La . . . and Nakeeda's right behind her. I guess we only need your dance buddy, and all your girls will be here."

He walked to the side so he could warm up. Stretching, locking, he got lost in the world in his head. This just wasn't any competition, it was *the* competition. He may've had his vending license and table, but that didn't guarantee the money he needed for school. Second semester was near, and he was short on the cash for it. In fact, he was behind for this month's tuition.

"You got this, Star."

Ziggy turned and smiled. He couldn't believe Broke-Up had shown. It was surprising enough that during the conversation on the corner, he'd asked if he could mix Ziggy's music, but Ziggy would've never dreamed his brother would come out to support him. He didn't think he was comfortable enough with the boy-from-the-family-dancing thing. "Thanks, Broke-Up," he began. Then his named was announced. "Showtime."

Ziggy flowed like water moving downhill. His moves were fluid; then he switched up, surprised everyone, including himself. He'd infused crunk dancing with be-bop swing, then transitioned to hip-hop ballet as if it were really a form. *No stopping me now. I got this.* "Harder," he whispered, pushing himself through a difficult move. "He can't beat you. No one can."

The sound of applause roaring in his ears when he'd finished his number told him he was right. Mrs. Allen walking up to him with the slightest smile on her face said everything he needed to hear. He'd won.

"Because I love this school so much, I'm going to donate some of my vending profits in the future," he said to her.

She smiled. "You don't have to do that, Ziggy. We appreciate it though."

The judges stood, and Ziggy straightened his shoulders waiting for his name to be announced in the top spot. He nodded as someone took third place. Smiled when a girl got second. Held his breath and waited for his name to be called for first. Then froze.

"We have a tie for first place between Kismet and Z. We'll need to—"

"Dance off!" Ziggy yelled, demanding. He wasn't just going to stand there and let his fate rest in the hands of the judges. He refused to win like that. If he was going to take first, he wanted to really take it.

The judges hovered and deliberated again, clearly concentrating as they ignored the chants of "Dance off! Dance off!" from the crowd. Seconds seemed like hours; then the head judge stood and turned to face the teenagers.

"There's been a mistake. A miscount. Z is the runner-up, Kismet is the winner," he said, but Ziggy heard something different.

"A miscount. Z won't be a student at Harlem CAPA because he now can't afford tuition. He not only lost out on the prize money, he blew any chance for a dance scholarship. Losers don't get scholarships, echoed in his head.

32

JAMAICA-KINCAID

Jamaica slid on her pants, stepped into her shoes, then tousled her locks. Quietly, she cleared her throat, not wanting anyone to hear. Carefully, she inched open the door, and looked up and down the hall. It was clear, she hoped. She hadn't been able to fully see because she couldn't open it all the way or stick her head out. As if she was coming out of the most normal place in the school, Jamaica walked out of the old storage closet, and hiked her book bag over her shoulder. Since she'd run from her parents, she'd been living in the school because she knew they'd track her; her address was somewhere in her laptop bag she'd left behind in the limo, she was sure. She'd written it on something for some reason, but it didn't matter anymore. All that counted was that she stay away from her old building, which also meant from Mateo's too. He'd insisted she could stay with him, but Jamaica didn't want to take any chances.

The bell rung, and most of the girls cleared the rest-room. Jamaica walked to the nearest sink, whipped out her toothbrush and paste, and began to brush her teeth. The mirror told her her eyes were red, and that she wasn't sleeping well in the closet. But she knew that already. She could've been put up in the Waldorf, and she still wouldn't have slept. How was great sleep possible when you were on the run and on a mission?

"Are you at least *bathing* here?" Mateo asked, walking into the girls' bathroom like he owned it.

She turned her head, and paste ran down her chin. She nodded, said, "After gym." She rinsed, then washed her face in the sink.

"Good. *You* look like—"

"Don't say it. Please. What's up, Mateo?"

He walked up behind her, and placed his hands on her shoulders. In the mirror they looked like a cute couple. But that was all. They'd never be together. She loved him like a brother, and was certain she cared more for him than her sister. "I was *only* going to say you look like you belong on *stage*. Ready?"

Her eyes went to the clock on the wall. The big round silver and white one every school had. It was time. She'd stayed up rehearsing lines all night, had slept until lunch, and now it was time for a run through of the play's lines before tonight's opening.

"Jamaica-Kincaid Ellison and *Mateo*?" Ms. Reed stood in the doorway, clearly shocked to see Mateo in the girls' bathroom.

"*Ma*teo who?" he asked, flashing out of the bathroom as if he'd never been there.

Jamaica turned. "Yes, Mrs. Allen?"

Mrs. Allen shook her head. "Don't 'Mrs. Allen' me, young lady. Follow me to my office. We need to talk. We do not house runaways here at Harlem CAPA."

Jamaica's heart fell, and she knew what she had to do. "Yes, Mrs. Allen," she said, following behind the director's hard steps. She shot Mateo a look, then swept her eyes for the exit door. *Run*, she mouthed, then took off leaving nothing behind but wind and Mrs. Allen yelling for her to come back.

The panties, the freaking crotch riders were riding up her rear and cutting into her skin. Jamaica now knew why the other actress was upset, had showed out, and lost her spot. If she wasn't performing in front of hundreds of people, she'd hook her index finger inside the elastic on her butt cheek and pull out the wedgie, and tell Talia to wear them. Nah, she told herself. No, she wouldn't. This was her moment. The first major play of her life, and she wouldn't trade it for the extra breath it would take for her to live forever.

"It's a shame, really . . ." she began her lines, then trailed off when she saw her parents in the second row. How did she not see them earlier? ". . . the way they make these undies," she continued, catching herself before the audience sensed her hesitation and that she'd almost messed up. She smiled. Although she was scared, and hated that she'd obviously been found, the pause in the lines made them stronger. It was an artist's license to enhance the scene, and that's what she'd done. Her other lines came off without a problem, and she'd said them as if they weren't rehearsed or memorized. Then she quickly made her exit off stage right.

"Bravo!" her father said, meeting her around the back. "So this is what you were doing? You've been here in New York all along . . . and *alone*, because this is your dream." He was in motivational mode.

"Dah-ling, why not tell us? Why rough it? Jamaica, I'm very disappointed in you. Very." Her mother chastised her, then drew her into a big comfortable hug. "But you were good. Very good."

"How did you know?" Jamaica asked, her face pressed into her mother's shirt.

"Me, of course!" Talia said.

Jamaica turned, and was face-to-face with the director. "You?"

Talia smiled, then walked over to Jamaica's mother. The two linked arms. "We go way back. College buds."

Jamaica's eyebrows crinkled. Now she was angry and embarrassed. She wanted to make it on her own merit. She wanted to land the part because she was good, not because she was her parents' daughter. "How could you do that? You set me up, and made me think I was good enough."

Talia laughed. "Jamaica, my dear, you are good. One of the best young actresses I've seen in a long, long time."

She looked at her father. "So this means I can stay in New York, right?"

"No."

33

LA-LA

"You know I'm going to beat this, La-La," Remi said as the cab pulled up to their project. "I don't know what you're so scared of."

La-La looked at her sister in awe. "You're not even a little scared, Remi?" She paid the driver, opened the door, then helped Remi out.

Remi laughed. "Scared of what? I've already been through the worst, and, truthfully, I wasn't afraid then." She shrugged, then walked toward the building. "I mean, really, I only had two choices, right? Chemo or death. I was more afraid of the needle."

La-La choked on air and Remi's confession. How could she be so strong? "So you never considered . . . ?"

Remi shook her head. "And you shouldn't be afraid either."

"Afraid of what, Remi?"

Remi stopped and looked La-La in the eyes. "Of Nakeeda. Of going after Ziggy when you like him so much. You shouldn't be afraid of making it, La-La. I think that's what you're scared of, becoming a big star and having to face what you want more than anything. It has nothing to do with your teeth." She put her hands on La-La's shoulders. "If you were afraid of people staring at you, you wouldn't have cut your hair to make me feel better about not having any."

All La-La could do was nod. Her sister was right about her. She was afraid. She feared that she wasn't strong, good, pretty, or talented enough to go head-to-head with her competition, win the boy, and become as famous as everyone said she would. "I love you, Remi."

Remi rubbed her hand over her head, and batted her eyes. "Of course you do, La-La. How couldn't you, with all this beauty and brains, and this crystal ball?"

La-La pushed open the chorus room door and entered the hall. To her left, Nakeeda and Hammerhead-Helen were talking loudly as usual, and La-La decided it was now or never. She was tired of being Nakeeda's target, and thought it was time she checked her. If Remi didn't fear dying, why should she let Nakeeda intimidate her? The answer was she wouldn't. Not anymore. She was no longer afraid of anything, and it was better to do something while scared than not do it at all. Pivoting, she turned and walked toward hell to face Lucifer and her she-devil.

"Well, look who it is. Baldilocks number two," Nakeeda said to her flunky.

Hammerhead-Helen laughed. "Where's Ziggy? Oh, I forgot . . . sorry."

Before La-La knew it, her hands were wrapped around Nakeeda's throat, and she was pushing her against the lockers. "Let me tell you something, Ms. Get Down and Around With Anyone. You will never use those words again. Are we clear? My sister is not a baldilocks, she's a better person than anyone you know. And you won't talk to me like that either. I'm not afraid of you."

Nakeeda pushed La-La off her. Her action said strength, but her eyes gave away her inner feeling. She was scared. "Get off me."

La-La pushed her back. "I'll tell you what, since you want to test me, test me."

"Hunh?"

Hammerhead-Helen crossed her arms, then stepped back. It seemed that, like Nakeeda, she was all mouth too. All words and no action.

La-La stepped so close to Nakeeda they were exchanging breath. Her exhale became Nakeeda's inhale. "You want to be me so badly, want to beat me so badly, want my boyfriend so badly that you'd go trick off your baby's Similac money to buy him dance shoes"—she flinched toward Nakeeda like she was going to hit her—"but you won't sing against me."

Nakeeda rolled her eyes, but was looking the other way. "Whatever."

"No 'whatever.' *Wherever.* I'm ready when you are. We can do this right here, right now."

The hall thickened with teenagers, and their appearance seemed to fuel Nakeeda's fake swagger. "All right. We'll sing then, and the winner gets Ziggy and the school."

La-La reared back her head. "What do you mean?"

"I mean whoever wins gets to date Ziggy and stay at the school, and the loser has to transfer."

La-La closed her eyes, and gulped. She had once been sure she could beat Nakeeda, but was she possibly wrong? There was no way Nakeeda would make such a bet unless she had a trick up her sleeve. But she was tired of being afraid, sick of running. If Remi wasn't scared of anything, neither was she. "Deal."

Nakeeda and Hammerhead walked away laughing. "Guess she don't know you've been taking lessons and joined the choir," Hammerhead-Helen said loudly enough for La-La to overhear.

She hung her head and shook it. She knew there was a catch.

34

REESE

The music room was filling up with students as Reese walked around it to the soundproof studio housed in the back. The teacher cleared his throat, calling out for Reese's attention. Without thought, she reached inside her pocket, pulling out her permission slip before she reached him. She had clearance, even against her mother's wishes. It was her supplemental time, and she was free to create any way she liked. That was school policy. He looked at the paper, scribbled something on it, then handed it back to her.

"You must be pretty good to know how to work that board," he said, a slight smile on his face. "I may need to hear what you're working on one day, and maybe you can show some of the other students how to use the equipment."

She smiled pleasantly. He could check on her now if he wanted, he could even engineer as far as she was concerned. But she knew what she was doing. She'd been sneaking and doing it forever, so she was even better when she was able to be all that she could be and not worry about getting caught or a watchful eye.

Pulling open the door, she flicked on the lights and set down her bag. She cleared her throat. "You can come out now," she whispered. "It's all clear."

"You sure?" Broke-Up whispered from behind the shelves where the old reels and other equipment were stacked.

"Yes. I got clearance, and the music teacher signed off. Come out. We don't have much time."

He crawled out on his hands and knees, and had some sort of cover on his back. From a distance, he resembled a piece of moving furniture. "You know how long I've been in here? Seems like hours." He jumped off, dusting himself off. "Time to get to work. By the way, what are we working on?"

Reese smiled. If she couldn't count on anyone else, she could count on Broke-Up. She'd called him, begged him to sneak into the school's music production room, and hadn't told him what for. Still, he showed. "I thought we'd put together a mixtape. It'll be good to shop, and we can use it to raise money for the school. More specifically, we can use it to raise money for a production program."

"Cool, Star. Let's get it poppin'."

They plugged in plugs, adjusted volumes, sequenced, mixed, and created. Together, they were fantastic. Music pumped out of the speakers, making them both bounce their heads. Reese knew there was nothing they couldn't do. Yes, they'd caught the hip-hop bug, but who knew what other sounds they were able to master? Rock. Pop. Country. Blues. Reese was ready to do it all. She wouldn't limit herself, that's the oath she'd taken. If she could've dug Mozart up from the grave, she would've remixed his work until he danced to it in clubs. Her phone vibrated on her hip, and she ignored it. She didn't have time to talk. She only had time to do. Again, it buzzed, and wouldn't stop.

Finally she answered, "Hello?"

"Reese. Messiah here."

She reached for the board to turn down the volume so she could hear him. "One sec, let me turn this down."

"Nah. Reese, turn it back up. I like what I'm hearing." He paused. "And obviously so does someone else."

"Hey, Reese. I see you're still making those hot tracks," the superpower artist she'd had the pleasure of working with said. "Who's it for? I told you my album isn't complete."

Reese smiled, then elbowed Broke-Up. She offered him part of the phone so he could hear. They stood head to head while she told Messiah and Ms. Superpower what they were doing.

"Really?" Ms. Superpower asked. "Mind meeting me at the studio later? I'd like to sing on that . . . if you don't mind. I always wanted to go to that school, but I was in Texas then, on the road."

Broke-Up jumped up and down, swinging his arms, and his leg was popping. Reese covered the mouthpiece of the cell. She didn't want Messiah and Ms. Superpower to know how open and excited she was. Yes, they could come down. Yes, she could sing on the track. And, yes, she and Broke-Up had just made it. They were official, and, if the school did nothing else, it'd have to allow music production.

35

ZIGGY

"Hurry up, everybody!" Ziggy yelled, excited. His enthusiasm contradicted with the nervousness bubbling in his stomach. He took a seat on the sofa, palmed the DVD remote, then turned it over and over again in his hand.

"Stoppit," Broke-Up urged. "He gonna know something wrong because you keep acting like a nervous little girl."

Ziggy looked at the remote, then set it next to him.

Their mother made her entrance first, wiping her hands on her apron. She'd been in the kitchen making roti, and wasn't too happy with being interrupted. "What is it, Ziggy? Why the yelling? You're not outdoors, ya know?"

He patted the empty place next to him on the sofa, asking her to sit. And then the living room took on a dreary tone. Pop walked in. He had a Guinness in his hand, and a half-scowl on his face.

"What is it? Somebody got shot or something? Yelling in the house like that. Boy, you know better."

Broke-Up cleared his throat. "Pop, sit down for a sec. We got something you need to see."

Ziggy was glad that Broke-Up included himself. That'd make it easier because it showed that he was supported.

Pop leaned against the doorway, crossed one ankle over the other, then swigged his drink. That was his way of saying: *You've got my attention.*

Broke-Up took the cue, got up, then pressed PLAY on the DVD player.

Ziggy held his breath, readying himself for the blow to the chest he was sure their father would deliver right before he kicked him out of the house. The music began, the video popped onto the screen, and a little of Ziggy's confidence died.

"Me no wan to 'ear dis—" Pop ranted in his island tongue.

"Pop! Please," Ziggy said, stopping him. "Watch please."

And there he was. Ziggy. On the screen dancing. Alone.

"What the hell? Ziggy, is that you?" Pops asked at full volume.

Their mother gasped, then put her hand to her chest as if she were having a heart attack. Ziggy almost panicked, then noticed a smile part her lips. She was enjoying it. Proud.

"Ziggy! Broke-Up! What is this rasclot . . .?"

The girl was dancing with Ziggy now. His hands were on her hips, gripping them as if she belonged to him.

"Hmm," Pop mumbled.

Ziggy got up and turned off the video. He knew he could've just stopped it from the sofa, but he needed to stand. If he was going to stand against his father, he'd have to do it like a man. When his father was silent, he knew what to do.

"Well, I'll pack my stuff now."

His mother stood, hands on hips. "What'chu mean 'pack,' Ziggy?" Her eyes went from Ziggy to Pop to Broke-Up, then to Pop again.

"Pop is against dancing—"

Now she was irate. "I don't give a care what he's against, or anybody else for that matter. My son,"—she pointed to Ziggy and Broke-Up—"aren't leaving this house because of no dancing or anything else."

For the first time in Ziggy's life he saw his father worried. He didn't know whether to celebrate or feel bad for him.

Pop sucked his teeth, then swigged the Guinness. He looked at Ziggy. "You like boys?"

Ziggy's chest inflated. "No. I don't like boys."

Pops nodded. "You know dancing is gay . . ."

"I'm not gay, Pop!"

". . . but, that dancing," he said, nodding. "Isn't too bad. Especially with the girl."

"Just because I like to dance doesn't mean I don't like girls. I'm a man, Pop." He banged his fist against his chest. "I've been hiding my dancing for years, and I'm tired of it. I pay for private school, go on auditions—"

"Shuddup, Z," Broke-Up yelled, cutting his rant short. "Didn't you just hear Pop?"

Ziggy cocked his head to the side. No, he hadn't heard anything.

Pop stood his full six-feet. "I said, 'That dancing isn't too bad. Especially with the girl.' "

Ziggy almost hit the roof from excitement. "Really? So you don't mind? I choreographed that. I want to choreograph videos back home in Jamaica."

Now Pop's excitement matched Ziggy's, but he checked it. "Not bad. Not bad." He nodded. "Wait till I shut my friends' mouths and that stupid Sandman. My son's not a dancer. He's a choreographer, and will be a Jamaican legend."

Good, thought Ziggy. Everything was coming together. Well, almost. Now he just had to find a way to get back into the school and win La-La back.

36

JAMAICA-KINCAID

Jamaica lay across the navy sheets with her feet dangling off the mattress. Her eyes were closed and her thoughts were vivid. She'd had so much fun in New York "making it" that she doubted she'd ever be happy in Connecticut or anywhere else. A cool rag placed across her forehead snapped her out of her miserable glee. That's what she had, confusion for feelings.

"So, you're *leaving* me, hunh?" Mateo stood over her.

She exhaled. "Yes and no. I'll be here for the summer programs, but I have to go back to that horrid boarding school for regular school." She grabbed the towel from her forehead, and dabbed at her eyes. She didn't want to cry.

"Don't go soft on me *now*. You did *it*, Jamaica. You *made* your dreams happen. How many people get to say *that*? And at your age?"

She looked at her best friend in New York, batting

back tears. She forced herself to smile. "*We* did it, Mateo. *We*. Me and you. You hooked me up, introduced me to the right people." She sat up, and crossed her legs.

Mateo sat down. "Yeah, *but* look at it this way. It was you, really. I couldn't *make* you do anything. *And* . . . because of you, Harlem CAPA won't close. I didn't know your dad was paid like that! *And* . . . because of you, I get to stay in a *swanky* apartment during the summer. Did you say they *bought* the apartment so you could live there while you take acting here?"

She nodded.

"Whew. I met the right friend!" He laughed. "But I'm going to miss you, rich white girl with blond locks," he said.

Jamaica wrapped her arms around him. "I'm going to miss you too, super-fine Spanish boy from the hood who inflects his words."

37

LA-LA

La-La paced back and forth waiting for Nakeeda to show. It had been an hour. A whole sixty minutes, and neither she nor Hammerhead-Helen had shown her chip-tooth or huge head.

"So, you know what this means, right?" Cyd said.

La-La nodded. "Yep. I win. But this is not how I want it. I want to spank that tail and make her cry. I'm going to show her."

The small audience of students clapped, and La-La looked up, certain that Nakeeda had shown her face. But there was no Nakeeda; they were clapping for her.

La-La grabbed the mic, turned it on. "Well, since y'all came here for a show, I'm going to give you one."

"Sandman! Sandman! Sandman can!" he yelled from his soapbox, laughing when he looked at La-La and Cyd. "What'chall doing 'round here?"

La-La laughed, she couldn't help herself. The ever-present Sandman always had something to say. "Good afternoon, Mr. Sandman."

"Yeah. Afternoon," Cyd added, giving him a pound as if he were their age.

Sandman stepped off his soapbox, tipped a non-existent hat, and bowed. "You know as long as I been mayor here, I don't think I've ever met more polite young-ins." He bent over, and dusted his wing tips. "I believe you two will make it. Harlem won't each ya alive. I won't let her, and she'll listen to me because she's my old lady."

"Thanks—" La-La began, then was silenced by a sharp pain to her ribs. "Ow!"

"There's your girl," Cyd said, pointing.

"Uh-oh. That's trouble in her mammy's shoes. Stay clear of her. She's one of them trouble-brewing statistics," Sandman added.

"Nakeeda!" La-La yelled. "Yeah. You. Thought we were having a sing-off? Bring it." La-La stepped up.

"Contest? Sing off?" Sandman got back on his soap-box, and announced the competition to the residents of Harlem. "Come get yo free show, better than *Showtime at the Apollo.*"

Reluctantly, Nakeeda dragged her feet toward them. Her eyes were rolling, and her arms were crossed, but she wasn't scaring anyone.

"You first," La-La said.

"Go ahead and beat her," Hammerhead-Helen urged.

Nakeeda opened her mouth, but nothing came out. "You go."

La-La cleared her throat, then turned to Sandman.

"Keep count of the witnesses, and judge us by hand-claps." She then turned, walked up on Nakeeda, then opened her mouth, and the most beautiful melody floated out. Her voice was so powerful that Nakeeda ran off. La-La nodded when she'd finished. "Now, I've won."

Sandman tipped his invisible hat again. "Yes, you did. And I declare today your day."

38

REESE

"Yes, yes, y'all! To the beat, y'all. Party and move your feet, y'all." Reese stood on the stage with a mic in her hand, waving her other one back and forth in the air. Broke-Up served as the hype man, running from one side of the small stage to the next, getting the audience excited. They'd decided to have a party to sell their autographed mixtapes that were freshly pressed on CDs, and try to raise money to help save Harlem Academy.

Her father stood up front in the audience with his hands raised and swaying. Old as he was, the music industry had kept him in and cool. She didn't have to worry about him embarrassing her. Beside him, to everyone's surprise, stood her mother. She was angry and stuffy, but she was there. She didn't appreciate being strong-armed, but right was right, and she was wrong. She had no reason to deprive the students of an art because she didn't like it. Arts were important and needed in the world and schools.

"Hold your dollars in the air now," Broke-Up yelled. "If you want the school to stay open, we have to give, give, give. The government's not going to pay for it. New York City can't afford it—or so they say. So it's up to us! And we can do anything. Right?"

The audience roared.

Reese smiled, strutted back and forth across the stage, then pivoted. She took her place behind the piano, adjusting the mic so her keys could be heard. Then the hip-hop music stopped flowing through the speakers, and Reese began. Her fingers were on fire, caressing the ivories and tickling the blacks. Closing her eyes, all her energy flowed from her fingertips and made the grand sing and hum as if it were a person and not a Samick. Suddenly, she stopped and stood. All eyes were on her, and that's just the way she wanted it. She began nodding her head to music that wasn't playing, and the audience had a look of surprise and *what's going on?* on their faces. Then Reese's big surprise of the night walked on stage, and the people lost it. They yelled, screamed, and some cried.

Ms. Powerhouse walked over to the piano with a mic up to her mouth. "Good evening! Everyone give your girl Reese here a big round of applause, and Broke-Up too. They've done this for you," she said, then began singing.

Reese sat down and started playing again. Broke-Up hyped the crowd. Mrs. Allen's eyes started to tear, and Mr. Allen couldn't have been more proud, his smile told on him. Reese looked at her parents. She was sorry for all of her lying, but she wouldn't change it. Wouldn't change it for anything. She was Reese Allen, producer on a Julliard track.

It would be a stretch, but Reese was sure they could raise enough for CAPA to stay open. So far, they were short, but it was okay. Ms. Superpower promised that she and her rap mogul husband would donate the rest of the money. Still though, Reese and Broke-Up had wanted to do it on their own. It was a way to keep the school open, start a music production program, and try to get Broke-Up in.

He shrugged. "No problem, Reese. We tried."

"Try isn't enough. We need to get you in. You can't sell on One-two-five forever, plus the school has a good academic program. You're smart, Broke-Up. You need to be in school."

He nodded, then adjusted his fitted NYC hat. "I know. I go to school here and there. It's no big deal. Anyway, we have some money coming in from those tracks."

"Okay, whatever you say. But it still won't be enough for you and Ziggy's tuition and the equipment we need. And we need equipment. Badly. We can't use the production room for profit. They said if we do that again, it's bye-bye."

They put the money in their pockets, then walked arm in arm. It had been a long night, an even longer week, but it'd been eventful and worth it. She was glad she'd gone to the vending table that day, happier that she'd taken a chance on him despite Wheez and her mother being against her working with him.

"Yo, Reese?" Broke-Up said, coming to an abrupt stop. "Can I ask you something?"

Reese stopped next to him, almost tripping because her feet halted so quickly. She turned, looked into his eyes. The tone of his voice said his question was important. "What's that?"

He stepped forward, looking down at her. "So we have this whole production thing worked out, right? And we're working on getting the production program in Harlem CAPA. We've even established that we're going to find a way to get me in, and be able to pay for me and Z."

She nodded to each thing he said, still waiting for the important question.

He kicked his good foot, then shifted. His knee popped, but he didn't seem to notice or care. "So I was thinking . . ." he drifted off, letting his words hang in the air.

"Thinking what, Broke-Up?"

". . . that maybe . . ." He reached forward, and pulled her into him. "This." He kissed her.

Now there was a different kind of music playing in her head. A melody with an infinite loop, and she hoped it would go on forever.

EPILOGUE

And life goes on . . .

LA-LA

"Get off me, Lexus and Mercedes! Now!" La-La kicked her feet, trying to free herself from her siblings. She just couldn't understand why they didn't get it. She didn't have time. They were running late. She had to meet Ziggy on One-two-five to pick up some gift he'd bought her, and then be at a rehearsal after school.

"You need help?" Remi pushed in the room, wrapped her arms around Lexus, and pulled her until they both fell back and slid across the slick floor on their butts.

"Thanks, Remi. I'll be back here as soon as I can. Cool?"

Remi smiled. "No problem. I don't have radiation until tomorrow. You keep getting the days mixed up."

La-La nodded. Now that Remi was officially in remission, she'd mixed up everything, she was so happy. Grabbing her bag, she walked over and helped Remi up. "Later," she said, as she left, glad to know that for her sister there would be a later after all.

REESE

Clap. Clap. Clap.
Reese shook her head. There was no way this woman was still at it. Ever since Reese had pretty much strong-armed her mother into letting her produce, and gotten her to go to the board of directors about implementing a producers' program at the school, she made Reese pay dearly for it. It wasn't even five in the morning, and Reese had to get up. She had to practice. Had to, or all bets were off.

Lazily, she rolled out of bed, stomped to the bathroom, and sloshed water and a facial cleanser on her face. She couldn't wait for the day to pass because the quicker it did, the sooner it'd be tomorrow, and the faster tomorrow was here, the closer they'd be to getting Broke-Up into the school.

"Hurry. Hurry. Hurry. Reese! Don't forget we have a Julliard function to go to later. And, I guess you can take Wheez and Broke-Up. But not because I said so, that's your dad's doing."

ZIGGY

Traffic was a mess as always. Ziggy, angry and running late, zipped through the cars, almost getting hit once or twice. His life as he'd known it was over, but he'd get it back. By hook or crook, he'd make it happen.

"Hurry, Z! We're going to be late," Broke-Up said, passing him up.

Ziggy smiled. He may not have won the contest or the money, and he was too late to apply for a scholarship so there was no free ride for him, but he was happy. He would be back in Harlem CAPA before he knew it. Him and his brother.

"Z, you're going to like this school, Star. Lots of thick girls."

Ziggy shook his head. "Nah. I think I'm cool with La-La."

Broke-Up looked over his shoulder. "Smart man."

JAMAICA

Her yawn was big enough to swallow the Mississippi River. She hated her life. Couldn't stand the students, and found the teachers so boring. She wished she could have New York back. She missed her cheap cookies and boiled water, and she'd do anything to have Mateo in front of her now. But she knew it was impossible.

Her eyebrows shot up. Was it impossible? Her parents had bought an apartment in New York. So couldn't there possibly be a way for her to slip back in, maybe live there on the weekends? Jamaica sat back in her chair in the dreary room, looking at the boring hillside, and imagined what she could do. New York had possibilities, and she had a dream waiting for her there. She pressed her lips together, twirled one of her locks around her finger, and knew what she was going to do.

UPTOWN DREAMS

Kelli London

ABOUT THIS GUIDE

The following questions are intended to
enhance your group's reading of
UPTOWN DREAMS.

Discussion Questions

1. La-La, despite having a hard home life, an ill younger sister, and teeth she was ashamed of, still followed her dreams. Using La-La's despite-all-odds-dedication as an example, how far would you go to make your dreams come true?

2. In the beginning, La-La didn't want to sing or go to Harlem Academy of Performing Arts. What made her change her mind?

3. Reese was a talented musician whose instrumental abilities could've landed her in one of the best colleges in the world if she had followed her mother's wishes. Do you think Reese was selfish for wanting to go after her own dreams? Or could/should she have done both?

4. Reese and La-La's lives are two examples of situations where parents want things for them that they don't want for themselves. In your opinion, is that good or bad? Can/should there be a compromise?

5. Ziggy had to hide his dancing from his father because it went against his father's beliefs about what a boy should do. Do you think Ziggy's father was fair?

6. Ziggy was a ladies' man because he believed it would thwart some people's assumption that a male dancer is gay. Have you ever acted other than you are to make other people accept you?

7. Jamaica took a lot of risks to get what she wanted. She lied, manipulated, and even moved to another state without her parents' permission to become the actress she'd always dreamed of being. Though it's good to go after one's dreams, is there such a thing as going too far to get what you want? Was there another way Jamaica could've gone about it?

8. Like Jamaica, are you using your talents to secretly get what you want? If so, how?

In Stores Now!

Boyfriend Season by Kelli London

First boyfriends, first love, first mistakes—and an invitation to the hottest teen society party of the year— send three savvy girls into a tailspin. Can they handle the pressure of getting everything they think they want?

Turn the page for an excerpt from *Boyfriend Season* . . .

```
┌─────────────────────────────────────────────┐
│                                               │
│        SPECIAL INVITATION TO                  │
│     THE HOTTEST SURPRISE PARTY                │
│           OF THE SUMMER                       │
│                                               │
│                 For                           │
│                                               │
│            Santana Jackson                    │
│                                               │
│                  +                            │
│                                               │
│             One Guest                         │
│                                               │
└─────────────────────────────────────────────┘
```

The invitation was in her hands. Between her fingers, and Santana couldn't believe it. Yes, she'd always been hot, one of the few who pulled everyone's attention, but now that her life had changed, she hadn't expected to be invited to the biggest rapper of all time's surprise birthday party.

She looked at her dress, and felt more than beautiful—she was exquisite. She scanned the crowd, and saw the people matched the feeling soaring through her. Yes, she was still on top. Then she looked to her right, and sized up the guy next to her. He was her date, and now everyone would know—everyone who expected her to be dangling on the arm of someone else. She hoped they'd all understand and celebrate her decision. It was summer, after all, and after spring bloomed change. Change of clothes, change of heart, change of mind—and especially change of boyfriends. If summer wasn't anything else, it was definitely boyfriend season.

> **SPECIAL INVITATION TO**
> **THE HOTTEST SURPRISE PARTY**
> **OF THE SUMMER**
>
> For
>
> *Dynasty Young*
>
> +
>
> One Guest

Dynasty gripped her invite, and held on to her date for balance. She wasn't used to high heels or standing on tip-toe in search of some boy. But the guy she was looking for was different. Super fine, he'd swaggered his way down from New York to Hotlanta, and stepped straight into her heart—just as she'd accidentally slipped into her date's—without trying. So was it her fault that she was digging one guy and had shown up at the most blazing party of the year with the one who dug her most? She shrugged. Her date was the greatest boy she knew, but they were friends. *Just best friends*, she told herself.

Fireworks exploded in the sky, catching Dynasty off guard. She jumped and almost fell. Then she saw him. The guy who had her heart. The same dude who had swaggered his way to Hotlanta and, apparently, into the heart of the girl he'd brought with him. Her name was Meka, and her swagger matched his. Dynasty blinked back her disappointment and swallowed her jealousy.

"You okay, Dynasty?" her date asked.

She looked at him, saw the beauty that lived behind his eyes, and thought, *Isn't this what every girl wants—her boyfriend to be her best friend?* She had a decision to make, and she decided it'd be tonight. It was the party of the year and, for her, boyfriend season.

SPECIAL INVITATION TO
THE HOTTEST SURPRISE PARTY
OF THE SUMMER

For

Patience Blackman

+

One Guest

Dear God. Thank you. Thank you so much, Patience prayed silently as lights flashed and microphones were thrust in her and her date's faces. She smiled a megawatt grin, and took in the positive energy surrounding her. Like the star everyone was now calling her, she stood tall on the red carpet with a real superstar next to her, and had not an ounce of remorse about leaving the one she'd left. She'd chosen the right guy as her date, she knew she did. So why was she so nervous about running into her ex? *Just nerves*, she told herself as anxiousness climbed her. She'd never been to a party before, hadn't ever attended a real concert, and now here she was, a church girl with an R & B/hip-hop record who was surrounded by celebrities and Atlanta's it crowd. No, Sunday service hadn't prepared her for this, not her new life.

"'Ey! You look good, Patience," her cousin, Meka, called through the crowd, pushing her way over.

Patience waved, and excused herself from her date. "Hey to you, too," she greeted her rowdy, but fun-loving cousin, then turned to Meka's best friend she hadn't seen until they were closer. "Hi, Santana! You look wonderful."

Santana grabbed Patience by both wrists, bopped up and down, and cut her a coy look. "Who's looking fab, superstar? I heard your song on the radio. Hot to def! I mean, it sounds really good."

Patience pulled away, laughing. "Thanks. I tried to do a lil something-something."

Meka laughed. "Patience, it's sumthin'-sumthin', not something-something. Don't worry, you'll get it." She stopped talking, and began waving her arm frantically. "Hey, Dynasty! Over here!" She turned to Patience. "Now this one you must meet. She's right up your alley. Good girl. Smart. Going places . . . and a little homely," she teased. "But you'll love her. I promise."

1

SANTANA JACKSON

Santana burst out of the classroom and into the hall. She couldn't take it anymore. Not the classroom. Not the students. Not the teacher or her rules. It was summertime. Boyfriend—Pharaoh—and boosting—clothes—season. She had things to do, and plenty of time as far as she was concerned. Well, at least now that she was skipping the rest of the day she did.

"This school can kiss my entire *asssk* me no questions and I'll tell you no lies!" Santana mumbled as loudly as she could, breezing past Beekman, the summer-school principal. She wanted him to hear her, just not be able to *prove* what she'd said. Cursing in the Atlanta public school system was forbidden—a major violation she thought ridiculous and refused to be penalized for. She didn't do detention, and had no plans of starting today.

She had more important things on her agenda like shopping and meeting her boyfriend, Pharaoh. Besides, if her mother didn't care what she said, who were the teachers to question what escaped her lips? Plus, being on lockdown in a classroom was raggedy with a capital *R*. But rappers, thugs, and corner boys—hustlers around her way who made things happen by connecting the dots—they were a different story. Who didn't want a dude who was saucy, could feed your pockets, stomach, and mind, and spat "shawty" through platinum and diamond grills covering his teeth?

Pausing in the middle of the hallway, Santana turned and mean-mugged Beekman, who'd quietly fallen in step behind her. She silently dared him to question her being in the almost desolate hallway during class time, then shrugged her shoulders in a what's-up-whatchu-wanna-do gesture. When she wasn't met with opposition, she mouthed *I didn't think so* to the principal's lack of action, then hoisted her book bag over her bra strap, swooped her index and middle fingers through her belt loops, and hiked up her too-tight jeans to cover her butt that Rashad, her neighbor, referred to as an onion. An apple. A badonka-donk that served as an asset in the hood. Then she exhaled, realizing she'd been holding her breath and that she had an audience. A smile tugged at the corners of her mouth when she noticed two boys staring. They were admiring what was beneath the denim separating their eyes from her juiciness, so she got her sway on, moved her hips like a pendulum while their eyes followed the switch of her hips. She was fly and knew it.

"A'ight, Santana!" they greeted with a head nod.

"Yep." Santana threw up the deuces and kept it moving. Yes, they knew her name, but so did just about everyone else in the school. She was Santana Jackson. Pharaoh's girl. And they were just fans.

Her phone vibrated in her purse as she pushed her weight against the door, exiting with a bang. It was almost one o'clock, close to their predetermined meeting time. Her feet lightened with each step as her shoes connected with the concrete beneath them. As always, she couldn't wait to see Pharaoh. Not only was he her dude, he was *the* man. His name rang bells, and his hood power preceded him. There wasn't anything that Pharaoh couldn't do—except Santana. She wasn't going to give in to him or be like one of the floozies who dropped their panties to guys because they were fly. She knew better and vowed to heed her mom's example: If you give a guy what he wants, he has nothing to stick around for, but if you give him just a smidge of what he wants, he'll stay for the rest.

" 'Bout time! I was just calling you. I thought I was gonna havta come up in there and jailbreak you," Meka Blackman, Santana's best friend, said, snapping closed her cell and leaning next to the door.

"I know, right? I tried to leave faster, but Principal Beekman was parading around like he running something, so I had to walk the halls for a minute," Santana answered as they left the grounds and turned the corner.

"So we scared of principals now?" Meka teased.

Santana shrugged and walked up to the passenger door of the borrowed pickup Meka was driving. "I ain't scared of nothing. But I'm not doing detention for nobody . . . especially not two days before summer school lets out—I'm not trying to risk doing a repeat. Ya heard?" Meka clicked open the locks with the car's alarm remote. Santana stepped up into the cab of the truck and asked, "How long you got this one?"

Meka stuck a key in the ignition, turned, and winked. Throwing the gear in DRIVE, she brick-footed the accelerator. "Until whoever's-this-is pays my brother. He must owe him big time 'cause the rims alone on this godda be at least ten stacks. Don't worry, I'll get you to your man on time. First we got biz to handle, though. Then after that I need to check on my cousin, Patience." The truck blew down the street on the ten-thousand-dollar rims, zooming faster than any speed limit in the country, blasting music. "You ready?"

Santana held on tight. "You mean your church cousin with all the money?"

Meka nodded, adjusting the radio dial.

"That's what's up. When's she hanging with us?"

Meka turned, and deadpanned. "Either when hell freezes over or heaven warms up. My uncle *The* Bishop Blackman ain't having it. He don't want our ways tarnishing his daughter!" She turned up the radio, nodding her head to the music.

"Turn that up! Is that Trill's new song, 'Talum'bout'? We godda cop us tickets to his next concert."

"Yeah . . ." Meka agreed, nodding her head to the song. "That's that ish." She turned up the radio. "Okay, enough. We got biz to handle." She muted the speakers when the hottest teen rapper's song went off.

"And I'm ready too. You got my silencer?" Santana asked, referring to her boosting bag, the one they'd lined with foil and magnets and others things that prevented store's security detectors from sounding off when they exited the store with stolen goods.

Meka smiled and took a sharp corner on Peachtree, headed toward Lenox Square Mall. "Nope. I didn't bring your silencer, sis. . . ."

Santana scowled.

". . . I brought you two. Your old one and a *new* one. Check in the back. Now fix your face! Over there looking like someone pissed in your cereal," Meka said, then laughed.

Santana joined her, then reached into the backseat of the truck and retrieved a big brown, recycled shopping bag. She was proud of her friend. "Even thieves are going green!" she teased.

"Ha-ha. I made some extras this morning 'cause I got orders to fill," Meka continued while Santana pulled a new tote from the brown bag.

"This the new Gucci? Jungle tote? The two-thousand-dollar jammie?" Santana's jaw fell in her lap while she admired the bag.

"Yep. *And* it's a silencer. Merry Christmas in the summertime. Don't say I ain't never give you nothing," Meka rattled. "ADT, Brinks . . . Atlanta Police Department—they can all kick rocks. Ain't no alarms gonna ring with all the stuff I lined our bags with!" She laughed and whipped into Lenox's parking lot.

Santana hugged Meka as soon as they hopped out of the truck.

Meka shrugged. "Don't be too happy. It's a knockoff, but no one can tell. Not even the employees that work at the store. Trust me. I returned one knockoff last week."

The M.A.C. counter was calling her name when they entered the mall and walked past Macy's, but she knew she didn't have time to stop. She was there to "shop" for a few items, maybe pick up some new Js, and then meet Pharaoh out front. He was due to pick her up in less than one hour.

"Where you wanna hit first?" Meka asked, smoothing out her sundress, then her extra short hair that was styled to perfection as usual. "You need a new Louis, right?"

Santana walked beside her, shouldering her dressed-up boosting bag and rocking her black and purple high-heeled Air Jordan 8s. There wasn't a soul who could tell her she wasn't a showstopper. Pausing in front of a store window, she checked her reflection. Fingering the top of her hair that was expertly spiked in a Mohawk, she turned sideways and admired how her graduated length cascaded down her back. *Even if I didn't grow this, no one can tell me my hair isn't fire.*

"I do, but wrong mall. Louis is in Phipps Plaza across the street. You always forget."

"Right. Phipps. Too expensive and too much security for me. I'm not trying to get locked up again," Meka answered, capping her lip gloss and putting it in her purse, signaling she was done and ready. "You're cute. Come on," she added, interrupting Santana's beauty session.

"I know. You too."

Meka grabbed her wrist, then pushed Santana's hair from her face. "What? When did you get these," she asked, fingering Santana's earrings. "These are ultra hot!"

Santana blushed. "Pharaoh had them made for me. If

you look carefully, you can see Ps in the design," she squealed, proud of her man.

"That's what's up. He's claiming his woman! Now it's time to get to work." Meka tilted her head; then they both nodded. If they were going to boost, they'd decided long ago that they'd better do it dressed to the hilt so they would be inconspicuous. Being raggedy would make security hawk them.

A crowd of dusty teenage boys walked past them and headed back toward the entrance of Macy's. Rundown sneakers, last season's clothes, jeans sagging too low and voices talking too loud, they were definitely targets for mall and department store security. They were also the distraction Santana and Meka needed to keep them under the radar.

"Guess Macy's it is," Santana said.

Silencer bag filled to capacity, Santana exited the third store they'd hit and headed toward the escalator. Her adrenaline rushed, her heart raced, and she was sure she was shaking. It took every ounce of willpower she had not to turn around to look to see if they were being followed. She was nervous. *Just nervous*, she told herself.

"We need to go upstairs. That's where the Js are," Santana said, leading Meka through the mall, past the Starbucks, and finally to the escalator. "One of us needs to buy something. I'm gonna cop the Js for Pharaoh." She stepped on the ascending stairs, then turned around so she could check their surroundings while she was speaking to Meka. "We're good. Nobody's thinking about us."

Meka's expression was twisted. "Why you buying Pharaoh something? Shouldn't it be the other way 'round?" she asked, hopping off and following Santana.

Santana laughed, then entered the store. "Girl, nah. He always buys me stuff. A pair of Js ain't nothing. Plus, for what I'll get in return . . . it's a good investment. Anyway, I want my man to look good."

"Don't keep him looking too good. You know them floozies at your school be after him. Especially Nae."

Santana sickened. She couldn't stand Nae, her ex-best friend who'd gone after Pharaoh at a party. "Meka, forget it. Don't even bring it up. He don't want Nae. How could he . . . after this?" Santana swung her weave while strutting over to the men's sneaker section. She grabbed the new Js and Ones off the display, then asked a salesperson to bring her a size-twelve pair of each.

"Hmmm. Don't ever say what ya man won't do. K?" Meka said, following Santana to the counter.

Santana turned on her three-inch-heel Jordans. "Why Meka? Is that a warning or a hint? You know something? Talk to your girl, Meka!" she said, peeling off a few big bills, paying for the sneakers.

Meka eyed the money.

"Courtesy of Pharaoh." Santana took the bags from the salesperson.

Meka walked out, shrugging. "I'm just saying, Santana. Don't ever be so sure. K? Nae may not be fire like you, but, just like ya man, she gives courtesies too. Maybe not cash, but her courtesies rhyme with cash."

"And I'll kick her in hers if she tries me again," Santana pointed out as they exited the mall. "There's

Pharaoh's car over there. I'll call you later, Meka." She blew her best friend air kisses, then sashayed toward her man. " 'Ey, baby!" Santana waved and cheesed so hard she was sure her teeth would shatter. The wind swept her weave off her back and moved her closer to him.

Pharaoh played with the chew stick in his mouth, biting and turning and sucking on it as if it were sugarcane. He gave Santana a head nod, reached over and opened her door.

"S'up, shawty? You lookin' kinda right in dem there jeans."

Shaking her head, she put her bags in the backseat and suppressed the melting feeling that swept through her every time he was near. Pharaoh had a way of appealing to her senses, starting with his street talk. Everything he said, no matter how simple, was beautiful to her because she loved his ghetto-fabulous country grammar. Sliding into the seat next to his, Santana leaned her weight to the left until her shoulder touched his, then wrapped her arms around him and met his lips with hers, giving him a sweet peck. They could've shared a seat and, still, she couldn't be close enough.

"Thanks. You what's up. Where're we going?"

Pharaoh roared the Charger's engine and spread his soft lips into a sneaky smile, revealing a platinum and rose-gold grill.

"Er'where Shawty. Ya know? If you still rollin'." He threw the gearshift in drive, released the brake, and accelerated until their heads indented the headrests like they were on a roller coaster.

Santana powered down her window, letting the warm

Atlanta air flow in and the blaring music out. She bopped her head, reached over, and ran her palm over his arm, loving the way his skin felt on hers. It was intoxicating knowing how powerful her man was. *There's nothing he can't do.* T.I. was rapping in the background. Paper-bag brown, fresh low cut with natural waves, he had just the slightest under bite that made his chin jut forward, causing him to look hard all the time. She took her hand, rubbed it over the hair he was growing on his chin.

"What up? You don't like that, shawty?" He looked over, flashed a slight crooked-tooth smile that revealed his platinum lower teeth, then stopped the car at the red traffic light.

She blushed. "You know I do." She reached in the back, retrieved the bag with his fresh kicks in it, then handed it to him.

He accepted the bag, then looked in it. He opened it and pulled out the Nike box first. A smile surfaced, followed by a low laugh. He nodded. "That's why I'm wit you, shawty. You a good girl and you know what it is. That's why I got a surprise for you too. Stick wit ya man, baby, and we going everywhere. Straight to the top, shawty."